The Forest of
Wool and Steel

www.**penguin**.co.uk

The Forest of Wool and Steel

NATSU MIYASHITA

Translated from the Japanese by Philip Gabriel

doubleday

TRANSWORLD PUBLISHERS
61–63 Uxbridge Road, London W5 5SA
www.penguin.co.uk

Transworld is part of the Penguin Random House group of companies
whose addresses can be found at global.penguinrandomhouse.com

Penguin
Random House
UK

First published in Great Britain in 2019 by Doubleday
an imprint of Transworld Publishers

Originally published in Japanese as *Hitsuji To Hagane No Mori* by Natsu Miyashita.
All rights reserved. English translation rights arranged with Bungeishunju Ltd
through le Bureau des Copyrights Français, Tokyo.

Copyright © Natsu Miyashita, 2015
English translation copyright © Philip Gabriel, 2019

Natsu Miyashita has asserted her right under the Copyright,
Designs and Patents Act 1988 to be identified as the author of this work.

Illustrations by Rohan Eason

A CIP catalogue record for this book
is available from the British Library.

ISBN 9780857525185 (hb)

Typeset in 11/14 pt Fairfield LT Std
by Integra Software Services Pvt. Ltd, Pondicherry

Printed and bound in Great Britain by Clays Ltd, Elcograf S.p.A.

Penguin Random House is committed to a sustainable
future for our business, our readers and our planet. This book
is made from Forest Stewardship Council® certified paper.

1 3 5 7 9 10 8 6 4 2

Contents

I

An Introduction to
Piano Tuning

Enter the Forest

I INHALE THE SCENT OF a forest close by. I can smell the earthy fragrance of autumn as night falls, the leaves gently rustling. I can feel the damp air of dusk descending.

The forest is not there. It is in my mind's eye. Because right now I'm standing in the corner of a deserted school gym at the end of the day. I'm a lower-sixth student and I've just accompanied a man with a large briefcase into the building.

In front of me is a black grand piano, a little grubby in places where it needs a polish. The lid is open. The man stands beside it. He glances over at me, but we both remain silent. He gently presses down on the keys and the scent of warm earth and whispering leaves rises up in my mind, drifting from beneath the open lid of the piano.

Night has deepened. I am seventeen.

∽

WHAT IF I HADN'T LINGERED in the classroom after school that day? What if the teacher hadn't chosen me to help? I'll never know. The second term of the year. Midterm exams were in full swing with after-school clubs suspended in favour of study and sleep, the corridors cool and still. I didn't feel like going back to the boarding house where I lived alone, and had planned to visit the school library.

'Sorry about this, Tomura,' Mr Kubota had said, 'but we have a staff meeting so I'll be busy. We're expecting a visitor at four o'clock. You just need to show him to the gym.'

I was often asked favours. People seemed to feel comfortable asking me. Perhaps I looked like an easy-going type, or perhaps I was just always available. It's true I had plenty of spare time. And on the horizon, I had only graduation and the search for a job to look forward to. This is what was filling my mind at the time, though there must have been other things, too.

The errands I ran at school were never serious ones – important people did those. Ordinary work was for ordinary people. I assumed that the visitor that day fell into this category.

'Who is he?' I asked.

'A tuner,' Mr Kabuto said.

I'd never heard this word before, and thought it might relate to the air conditioning.

I had more school tests the next day so I buried my head in a history book for a while, before heading over to the entrance. A man in a brown jacket was waiting, a large case in one hand.

'Are you here for the air conditioning?' I asked, opening the door wide for him.

'My name is Itadori. I'm from the Eto Music Shop.'

I hesitated, momentarily confused.

'I hear that Mr Kubota has a staff meeting today,' the man said. 'So, if you'd be kind enough to show me where the piano is?'

I nodded, placing the brown slippers we used for visitors on the floor in front of him.

I wondered fleetingly what he was going to do to the piano, although to be honest I wasn't that bothered. 'Please follow me,' I said, leading him down the corridor and noticing how very heavy his briefcase looked. What on earth might he keep in there? I walked him over to the piano in the corner of the gym. He laid his bag carefully on the floor and nodded to me. My cue, I thought, to leave. I turned to go.

The gym usually resounded with students calling out during volleyball or basketball and the screeching and thudding of trainers on the maple-wood floors. At this hour it lay quiet. Evening light poured in through the high windows, bathing the whirling eddies of dust in a yellow glow.

As I made my way back down the corridor, the sound of the piano halted my step. It was mellow and rhythmic. I took a breath and listened again. A repeated clanging and twanging, higher then lower, echoed in the gym. It is hard to describe. But my soul was suddenly filled with a nostalgia and longing – and something else I couldn't quite identify. I was taken aback. I crept quietly towards the gym and peeked my head through the door as the man went about his business. Feeling braver, I came closer. The man continued industriously, knocking and twanging. He moved around the piano and carefully lifted the huge black wing of the lid, propped it on the support stand, and pressed a few more keys.

It was then that I smelled the unmistakable scent of the forest at nightfall, felt I was on the very cusp of setting foot inside. I considered entering, but resisted. The forest after dark is dangerous, after all – or so children's stories tell us.

On the gym floor his large briefcase lay open to reveal a set of tools, the like of which I'd never seen before. What he was planning to do with them I had no idea, and suddenly I burned with the need to know. Questions pressed and whirled in my mind. I had no idea how to put my curiosity into words, still regret even now not having asked anything at all. I've revisited that scene so many times since. If I had spoken up then, I wouldn't have had to spend so much of my life in search of the answers.

I looked on, remaining perfectly still and silent, not wanting to distract this man from his conscientious work. In that moment, the piano appeared utterly majestic, awesome in its near-perfection. I'd listened to smaller pianos so often in my junior school days, and had sung along with them. But a grand piano like this, I had never heard, and now I saw it in a completely new light. With its great black wing flung open and its insides exposed, it seemed to offer up an intimacy. Not only was it the first time I'd heard such a sound, but it was the first time I had been so moved to my very bones.

It was the scent of a forest on an autumn night. In for the long haul, I placed my satchel on the floor and watched intently. Two hours passed without my noticing. The time of year – indeed the time of day – came into sharper focus. Early September, six o'clock on a crisp, clear evening. Some light still lingered from the town, but here in this secluded mountain village, the trees cut off the last of the sun. As the sound – soft, warm, deep, repetitive – continued to spill from the piano, I sensed the nocturnal forest creatures crouching silently nearby with bated breath.

'This piano's pretty old,' said the man eventually. 'It has a very gentle tone.'

I nodded, although I wasn't sure what he meant. Was this a good thing?

'It's a very fine piano indeed,' he said.

I nodded again.

'Must be because the mountains and fields were better, back in the day.'

'Excuse me?'

He wiped the black piano slowly with a soft cloth.

'Sheep in the old days ate better grass in the mountains and fields.'

An image drifted into my mind of the sheep, heads bent, leisurely cropping the pasture near the mountain home where I grew up.

'They used plenty of felt made from the wool of good sheep that grazed on healthy grass. Can't make decent hammers like this any longer.'

I had no idea what he was talking about. 'What do hammers have to do with pianos?'

The man gave me a look, then a faint smile broke on to his face. 'There are lots of hammers inside a piano.'

I couldn't imagine this at all.

'Would you like to see?' he asked, and I moved closer. 'When you hit a key like this . . .' *Tooo–nn*. The sound rang out in the big airy gym. A part inside the piano lifted up and knocked against a line. 'See, this hammer here strikes a string, and the hammer itself is made of felt.'

The same sound resonated again: *tooo–nn, tooo–nn*. I couldn't tell if that was a gentle tone or not. But in the forest, near the beginning of September, around six in the evening, it was now starting to get dark.

'Is something the matter?' he asked.

'It's so much clearer than before,' I replied.

'What is much clearer?'

'The scenery of the sound.'

The picture that it conjured was now so vivid in my mind, even more so than when he first touched the keys.

'Could the wood they use in pianos possibly be pine?' I asked.

The man gave a slight nod.

'It's from a tree called spruce,' he said. 'A type of pine.'

My confidence growing, I asked, 'Could this by any chance be from pine trees cut down in the Daisetsuzan mountain range?'

The dark forest balancing on the flanks of those mountains – the image and sounds resonated in my very soul.

'Actually it's from foreign trees. From North America, I believe.'

Oh. So much for what I'd imagined.

The man heaved up the piano lid and closed it carefully. Then he continued to buff up the shine with a soft cloth.

'I imagine you play?' he asked.

His voice was soothing and I wished with all my heart that I could respond with a *yes*. How wonderful it would be to play the piano, and express the sounds of the forest, the night, all manner of beautiful things.

'No, actually, I don't.'

I'd never even touched a piano.

'But you like pianos, don't you?'

Did I? I wasn't sure. Only today had I become properly aware of this instrument, for the first time in my life.

He didn't seem to mind my reticence. He finished his polishing, stowed away the cloth, and quietly snapped shut the lid of his case. Turning again to face me, he took a business card from the pocket of his brown jacket and placed it in my hand. 'If you fancy it, feel free to come and take a look at our pianos.'

Soichiro Itadori, Piano Tuner

'Can I really?' I asked.
'Of course.' Mr Itadori nodded, smiling.

∽

I COULDN'T FORGET THAT ENCOUNTER. And one day I did go to visit the music shop.

As I arrived, Mr Itadori was heading off to a client's home, so I walked out into the car park with him and attempted a direct appeal. 'Will you take me on as your apprentice? Please?'

Mr Itadori neither laughed nor showed any surprise. He looked me in the eye, an inscrutable expression on his face. Then, appearing to have come to some sort of decision, he placed his case on the ground, took out a notebook and scribbled in it with a ballpoint, ripped out the page and handed it to me.

It was the name of a school.

'I'm just a lowly piano tuner,' he said. 'I'm not in a position to take on an apprentice. If you're serious about studying tuning, I recommend this place.'

∽

AND SO IT WAS THAT I graduated from school and convinced my parents to let me go to this place for specialist training. How much my family understood about it all, I still don't know. The village in Hokkaido where I was born and raised offered only basic schooling, and once children finished compulsory education they tended to leave the mountains for the big cities. Some of the mountain children flourished away from home, while others felt overwhelmed by the large colleges and bustling crowds. Some would eventually drift back to the mountains, others would disappear for ever. Me? Well, I chanced upon the forest – an extraordinary place that the piano opened up to me – and I couldn't return to mountain life.

At eighteen, I left the mountains of Hokkaido for the first time in my life. The training course was based in a piano factory on Honshu – Japan's main island – and for two years I was one of only seven students, learning the techniques of tuning from morning till night. Classes were held in a warehouse of sorts, so it was blisteringly hot in the summer, freezing in the winter. We studied everything from repairing an entire piano to applying the exterior finishes. Assignments were challenging and I was worried that I might not pass them, so I stayed late every night, struggling to hone my skills. Many was the time I felt as though I'd set foot in the forest of my childhood nightmares, the one where if you got lost you'd never find your way back, and sometimes the darkness threatened to overwhelm me.

Despite all this, I still loved it. I never caught the fragrance of the forest wafting up from the pianos that I tuned myself, but I could never forget that first scent. I clung to its memory and somehow managed to complete the course. I couldn't play the piano, didn't have a particularly good ear, and yet I was able to tune the forty-ninth key, A above middle C, to 440 hertz. A mere two years of study, although it seemed such a long journey. By the end, I was able to fashion together the whole musical scale.

Along with my six classmates I managed to graduate, then returned to the city near my hometown and landed a job in a music shop – the very same place where Mr Itadori worked. I was in luck as another piano tuner had just moved on.

∽

THE ETO MUSIC SHOP WAS a small establishment – four tuners, a receptionist, a handful of people in admin and sales – and dealt primarily in pianos. The head of the company, Mr Eto, was rarely around.

I spent the first six months in training, answering the phones, managing the music classes, handling customers on the shop floor.

On the ground floor was the showroom with six pianos (four upright, two grand), a corner where we sold sheet music and books, two rooms for private lessons, and a smart little auditorium for intimate recitals. Most of the time I was in the office on the first floor.

The days were so hectic it was only at night that I got the chance to practise my tuning. When everyone else had gone home, I opened up the lid of a piano – my favourite being the smallest of the uprights in a rich, reddish mahogany – and an exquisite silence would settle over the room. I felt my consciousness expand, and yet there was a folding inwards, too. I struck the tuning fork, my nerves entirely focused and alert.

I had no trouble tuning the strings, yet something still felt off-kilter. I just couldn't make sense of the sound vibrations.

The numerical values met the required specs when I measured them with my tuning fork, but I could still hear them wavering. Piano tuners do so much more than you might think – it's not simply a case of reaching a particular fixed set of pitches, but of understanding the vibrations and interactions among and between the notes. And this was where I found myself stuck. It felt as though I was in a pool and struggling, barely managing to tread water instead of gliding through with sure strokes. Every night it felt the same.

I didn't see Mr Itadori much. He was rarely in the office, often out tuning pianos in concert halls or tuning the instruments of a whole list of customers in their homes. He'd go directly to visit his clients then head straight home at the end of the day, so sometimes whole weeks passed without my seeing him.

I desperately wanted to watch him in action tuning a piano and for him to give me some technical pointers, but more than that I wanted to hear how he would refine the timbre of a piano and the colour of its tone. My feelings must have shown, for one day, just as he was leaving for an appointment, he placed his hand on my shoulder and said, 'There's no rush. Take it slow and steady. Slow and steady.'

My efforts so far had been exactly that: a tremendous, dizzying amount of slow and steady. I was pleased that Mr Itadori was concerned about me, but I needed more. I ran after him as he was nearing the door.

'But *how* should I be slow and steady? How do you do slow and steady the right way?' I stood in his way, trying to catch my breath.

Mr Itadori gave me a quizzical look. 'There's no standard in this job that tells you if something is right or not,' he said. 'Best to be wary of that word "right".'

His friendly round face nodded a few times, as though in agreement with himself. He pushed open the door that led out to the car park. 'Just take everything as it comes, slow and steady.'

I lingered and held the door for him, wanting to make sure he had no other gems of wisdom to offer.

'Don't try to run before you can walk,' he said.

So slowly and steadily, whenever I had the chance, I would tune the pianos in the showroom. One piano per day. After tuning all six I'd go back to the first and retune it, changing the pitch. It'd be at least six months more before I'd be allowed to tune a client's piano by myself, but to my comfort I learned that my predecessor had taken even longer. He'd been with the company for a year and a half before being let loose on clients' personal instruments.

It was Mr Yanagi, my senior in the firm by seven years, who had filled me in. 'That student had done the full course at a piano tuners' training school,' he said. 'Some people are just better suited to it than others.'

It was terrifying to think that no matter how hard I tried there was a chance that I might never make it to the end.

'What's important for a tuner is more than just your actual tuning technique,' Mr Yanagi said, patting my arm with his stubby-fingered hand.

I wasn't confident of my own technique. I'd graduated from a rigorous training course, but had only just mastered the basics. When I had to work on a piano that hadn't been properly maintained, the best I could manage was to re-arrange the frequency of the discordant sounds and align the scales. No one would ever call my results beautiful. This was all I was capable of and it gave me sleepless nights.

With no conviction in even my most basic skills, there was no way I could accomplish the finer aspects of tuning.

Perhaps sensing my unease, Mr Yanagi broke into a smile. 'Don't worry about it. Just be bold. Nobody's going to trust a tuner who seems uncertain.'

'I'm sorry.'

'No need to apologize. So long as you appear to know what you're doing, you'll be just fine.'

He was far more experienced than I was, but never set himself up on a pedestal or showed any measure of self-importance and I was grateful for his attention. Having spent most of my life in a very small community, I found it hard to truly grasp how hierarchies functioned. I knew power dynamics existed that went way beyond my experience and understanding.

∽

I LIKEWISE TOOK A SLOW but steady meander through the canon of music composed for the piano. Until I'd graduated from school I'd hardly ever listened to classical music, so it was a whole new world for me. I was instantly hooked and fell asleep every night to the strains of a Mozart or Beethoven sonata or a Chopin nocturne.

I'd had no idea there was such a diverse repertoire of music – so many sonatas, concertos, ballads, preludes, scherzos, studies, impromptus – and all performed by the widest possible variety of pianists. I had no sense of degrees of merit. I would never have the time to compare them all, so set myself the task of simply listening to as much as I could, trying not to choose the same pianist twice. Just as a newly hatched chick thinks the first creature it sets eyes on is its mother, so I too grew attached to the first performance I heard of each piece. As far as I was concerned, that pianist was clearly the best. The performance might be quirky, might be an interpretation that played freely with the tempo and dynamics, but if that was the first version I heard, it became the gold standard by my reckoning.

Whenever I had a spare moment I'd stand in front of a piano, heave open its mighty lid and peer inside. Eighty-eight keys, each with one to three strings attached. The steel strings were taut, and I felt a jolt of excitement each time I contemplated the line of hammers, ranged across the action like an exquisite row of magnolia buds, just waiting to be used. The forest, with everything in perfect balance, was utterly beautiful.

And here was another thing: 'beautiful', like 'right', was a totally new word for me. Until I'd found the piano I'd never been aware of things that you might call beautiful, which is a little different, of course, from not knowing they exist. I recalled the milky tea my grandmother used to make me when I came home from school. She'd boil the tea in a small pan, then add the milk, transforming its colour to that of a muddy river after a downpour. I often used to imagine the fish swimming in the hidden depths of the pan. She'd pour out the tea and I'd stare fascinated at the way the liquid swirled around in the cup, half expecting to see a fin or the flap of a small tail. I recognized beauty in that now.

The delicate frown lines between the brows of a crying baby. The bare mountain trees beginning to bud, and the ecstasy of the moment when the tips of the branches reflect a reddish hue, casting a warm glow across the mountain.

The mountain on fire with these imaginary flames would stop my breath and fill my heart to bursting.

It liberated me to have a word for these things – for the trees, the mountains, the seasons. To call them beautiful meant I could take them out any time I wished, exchange them with friends. Beauty was everywhere in the world. I had just never known what to call it or how to recognize it – until that afternoon in the school gym, when it flooded me with joy. If a piano can bring to light the beauty that has become invisible to us, and give it audible form, then it is a miraculous instrument and I thrill to be its lowly servant.

Sisters Are Cool

I REMEMBER VIVIDLY THE FIRST day I went out to tune a piano. Autumn was on its way, the sky a spellbinding blue. I'd been working with the company for over five months. Mr Yanagi was called out to tune a client's piano and I was to accompany him as his assistant, although in reality I was less of an assistant than an observer. It was a good opportunity to study technique, of course, and how one interacted with clients – the back and forth between client and tuner.

It's fair to say I was a bundle of nerves when Mr Yanagi pushed the intercom button outside the entrance to the white block of flats. A lady answered and her voice seemed kind. The door buzzed open, and I calmed myself with the thought that we were here for the piano rather than for her.

We took the lift to the fourth floor.

'I'm looking forward to this one,' Mr Yanagi murmured as we strolled down the hallway.

The door opened to reveal a woman of about my mother's age. The piano was standing in the first room to our right, where a thick blue carpet covered the floor and luscious heavy curtains hung at the window – for soundproofing, I imagined. Two identical stools were arranged in front of the piano. The instrument itself was a gleaming black baby grand, expertly polished. Not a particularly high-end model, it was nonetheless clearly looked after with pride. When Mr Yanagi played an octave interval I could sense immediately that it was out of tune, only six months after the last tuning, which confirmed that it was regularly played.

Now I understood why Mr Yanagi had said he was looking forward to working on it. It was sheer pleasure to tune a piano whose owner loved it so much. Pianos want to be played. They are always open – to people and to music, ready to shine a helpful guiding light towards worldly beauty.

Mr Yanagi struck the tuning fork firmly on his black briefcase. A high-pitched tone rang out and the A above middle C resonated with it. *It's fully connected*, I thought. I should explain that each and every piano is distinct and individual, but all pianos are essentially connected. To tune the piano we manipulate the tension of the strings and adjust the hammers until they produce uniform vibrations of pure sound to link the instrument to the multiple musical sounds out in the wider atmosphere. In silence and with a serious look on his face, Mr Yanagi was ensuring that this piano could at any moment harmonize freely with the outside world.

As he was finishing the job some two hours later, a voice sang out from the entrance to the flat.

'I'm back!'

Moments later, a young woman of about seventeen stepped into the room. She had black hair down to her shoulders and seemed shy. She bowed slightly, first to Mr Yanagi and then to me, before leaning against the wall to watch silently as Mr Yanagi tapped away.

'Is this to your liking?' Mr Yanagi played two scales before stepping away from the piano.

The girl approached tentatively, and let her fingers glide gently and affectionately over the keyboard without answering. I felt goosebumps rise on my bare arms.

'Go ahead – play it, and see what you think,' Mr Yanagi said, gesturing encouragement. In silence, she pulled up her piano stool and settled down, placing her hands on her thighs for a few seconds before running her fingers lightly over the keyboard. A short piece, both hands travelling evenly up and down and in contrary motion. An étude to train one's fingers, I imagined. I thought it was exquisite. The notes were precise, elegant. My goosebumps did not go away and my heart contracted a little when the piece was over.

The girl rested her hands back in her lap, then nodded briefly. 'Thank you very much,' she said in a staccato manner. 'I think this will do.' Her voice was low and she did not meet our eyes.

'We'll be going then,' Mr Yanagi said.

'Oh, please wait a moment,' the girl said, looking up suddenly. 'My younger sister will be home soon, so would you mind holding on for her?'

It seemed odd that her younger sibling should have the final say, but I wondered whether in fact it said more about the girl in front of us and her own reticence.

As I pondered this, a beaming Mr Yanagi said, 'Happy to oblige.'

The girl left the room for a moment and her mother walked in carrying a lacquer tray. 'Please have some tea while you wait. If my other daughter doesn't come home soon, you really don't need to stay.'

She laid out the china cups and saucers on a small table in the corner of the room, and smiled, clearly anxious not to keep us too long.

Mr Yanagi halted the process of putting his tools away, always methodical. 'Thank you very much,' he said with a bow.

In less than five minutes the front door banged open.

'I'm baaack!' came a bouncy voice from the hall, and steps approached.

'Yuni,' called her sister, 'the piano tuner's here.'

'Oh good! Glad I got back in time.'

When they appeared together in the room, I was taken aback to see that their faces were nearly identical. The only difference was that one wore her hair down on her shoulders, while the other had hers in two braids hanging just below her ears.

'Have you already tried playing it, Kazune? If so, I don't need to.'

The younger sister – who I now realized could only be younger by a matter of minutes – stopped in the doorway and looked over at Kazune.

'No, you should definitely try it out. We like different things from our piano, you and me.'

The girl with the braids left the room again, while her sister with a slight bow explained that she'd be back in a moment. 'She's just washing her hands,' she said.

The other girl was soon back, her hair loose now so I could no longer tell them apart at all.

Although they looked exactly alike, the piano was a completely different instrument in the hands of this girl compared to those of her older sister. A different temperature. A different humidity. The sound was buoyant, overflowing with richness and colour. Now I understood why Kazune had insisted her younger sister play. With such variation in style, it would take a little finessing to tune the piano perfectly for them both.

The girl suddenly stopped and turned around.

'Can you make the sound any brighter?' she said. 'I'm sorry, it's rather selfish of me to ask.'

She was a tiny bit solemn in her expression as she said this, and over on the other side of the piano her older sister looked equally serious. I wondered if she too was hoping for a brighter sound. On perhaps she was simply deferring to her sister's opinion. The younger girl rose from her piano stool.

'I think perhaps you adjusted it so it didn't resonate as much? I think that suppressed the sound and made it a little darker.'

Mr Yanagi smiled and nodded. 'I understand. Let me take another look.'

He adjusted the pedals and set the dampers so they lifted more easily. And that's all it took for the sound, which had moments before been a little subdued, to be set free. In this small room it certainly felt brighter. But was that acceptable? The more strident tone fitted the younger sister's performance, but what effect would it have on her older sister's more serene style of playing?

The younger girl sat down to try the piano again after Mr Yanagi had adjusted it. 'Oh! It rings out so much more clearly now!' She stopped playing after a moment, stood up and gave Mr Yanagi an excited little bow. 'Thank you so very much.'

The older sister bowed in turn. Lined up side by side, they really were two peas in a pod, performing gestures in tandem. The younger one probably had the broader smile. The way each played the piano, however, was utterly and unmistakably distinct.

∽

THE SUN HAD ALREADY SET but the little white company car in the car park had grown warm and stuffy. Mr Yanagi placed his bag with his tuning tools on the back seat and opened the passenger door.

'So what did you think?' he asked as he squeezed into his seat.

I wasn't sure if he was referring to the sisters or the piano, and hesitated.

'The way she plays is always so delightful,' Mr Yanagi said, chuckling, his eyes creasing up with mirth. 'I haven't heard such spirited playing for quite some time.' He glanced over at me for a reaction. 'It was so passionate, don't you think? Makes it even more worthwhile tuning that piano.'

'I wish she'd played a proper piece, though,' I said. It was hard to tell if I could get away with showing any more enthusiasm.

Mr Yanagi shook his head vigorously so that a section of short black hair fell across one eye. 'That was a Chopin étude. It's short, but if she'd played anything longer we would have had to leave. We spent more time than was allowed in our schedule.'

A Chopin étude? I knew very little about classical music but could recognize some pieces, and surely that wasn't Chopin. *If anything, just a few finger exercises*, I thought. And then it hit me.

'Didn't the younger sister play the Chopin étude?'

Mr Yanagi turned to look at me from the passenger seat, wide-eyed and eyebrows raised. 'What? You mean – you prefer the way the *older* sister plays?'

I nodded. Of course I did. I could honestly say it had touched my heart. I had never heard music communicated with such emotion and poise in equal measure.

'But *why*?' He wasn't going to let this go. 'The older sister's performance feels quite banal. She's very precise, sure. But when it comes to flair, the younger sister has it in spades.'

Was the older sister's playing so banal? Perhaps my inexperience with the repertoire for the piano led me to think that an average player was properly talented. The image came to me again of a baby chick cheeping as it toddled after its mother. This had been my very first experience of going to tune a piano in a home, the very first time I heard a client play. Perhaps that was why it was so special to me?

No, it wasn't. I refused to think her playing was ordinary, it was undeniably superior. As far as I was concerned it was close to magical. It moved me, made my eardrums ring, sent pleasurable chills up and down my body. I would never ever forget it.

'Her playing is really quite extraordinary,' Mr Yanagi said. 'The younger sister, I mean.'

I nodded. The younger sister was good, her performance vivid and full of joy. Surely she'd had no reason to want the piano tuned to a brighter sound than it already had.

I pressed on the clutch and let down the handbrake slowly.

And then I understood. It wasn't for herself that she wanted the cleaner, more sparkling sound from the piano, but for her *older sister*, whose playing was somehow darker and more restrained.

'I get it,' I said suddenly, and Mr Yanagi shot me a glance.

'What? You're being very weird,' he said.

'Sisters are cool,' I explained.

Mr Yanagi laughed. 'Especially twins, right?'

'Yeah.'

'They're both good pianists, and they're both adorable,' he said cheerfully, stretching his feet out in the footwell.

Although I now felt even less confident of my ability to assess the quality of anyone's piano technique, it was the perfect first home visit. If I could continue to work along these lines, then I would surely keep on learning, slow and steady.

Tuning Is Like Cheese

THE BERRIES ON THE yew trees that lined the streets of the city were changing colour now, brightening everything with their rich gleaming reds and purples. When I lived up in the mountains, I'd long for the wild kiwi fruit and grapes to ripen so I could pop one of each into my mouth on my way to and from school every day.

'Is anybody going to eat these?' I asked Mr Yanagi as we walked along, side by side.

'Hmm?'

'I wondered if the trees along these roads are considered public property? Are we allowed to pick the berries?'

'What do you mean?'

'The *onko*. Autumn's come late this year.'

As I was speaking I realized that city-dwellers had a different name for yews – not *onko*, but *ichii*.

'You know a lot about them,' Mr Yanagi said, sounding impressed. 'I don't know any names of trees. Where did you learn them?'

Well, I'd never consciously given it any thought. Certainly I grew up surrounded by trees, but only now did I realize I knew them by name. But, just like being able to tell salmon and greenlings and white-spotted char apart, this knowledge didn't amount to anything useful.

'I just know the names of trees, that's all. It doesn't serve any purpose.'

In the mountains it was much more useful to be able to tell apart the types of wind and cloud so you could accurately predict the changing weather.

Trees are trees. They are there whether I know their names or not, budding in spring, heavy with leaves in summer, laden with berries in autumn. When I was a child, playing in the woods on an autumn day, I'd hear the gentle plop of berries and acorns falling around me. It was a soothing sound. Just knowing they would fall whether I was there or not brought me peace.

I recall one particular time, when I had just turned ten, playing in the woods and thinking that even if I collapsed right at that moment and stopped breathing, the berries and the acorns would keep on gently dropping to the ground. It filled me with a curious sense of liberation, creeping up from the earth and through my feet. *I am free*, I thought. Then the wind turned, and cold and hunger sneaked up on me, and all at once I remembered the particular challenges of being human.

'You must know the names of flowers, too?'

The question pulled me out of my reverie. Flowers? I knew a few that grew in the mountains but none of the ones you find in a florist's.

'It's pretty cool to know the names of flowers,' he said.

'You think so?'

'I do. Not knowing things means you're not interested.'

I began to feel a little low as a result of this conversation. It was as though by discussing the trees and the flowers – things I had some knowledge of – the huge gaps in my musical knowledge were somehow widening. The client we'd just visited had asked me about a particular pianist's tone, a famous pianist by the sound of it, and I had been left floundering.

'What you see in the scenery is different from what I see,' Mr Yanagi said. I agreed. There were so many things I needed to notice.

'Any kind of knowledge is useful,' he said.

Was he trying to cheer me up?

'Do you mean in the sense that it's better to have plenty of topics to talk about, rather than just a few?' I ventured.

Mr Yanagi had a good reputation among the clients. Primarily, of course, because he was a skilled tuner, but being good at conversation was also important. He could follow any topic a client might bring up, and chime in intelligently. As for me, it seemed the best I could manage was to stand to one side and be awkward.

'Oh, I'm not talking about the art of conversation or being cultured or anything like that. But I think it helps with the essence of tuning a piano.'

The essence of tuning. I didn't understand what that meant. I was a mere apprentice, hovering on the periphery.

'Knowing specific names of things so you can picture the details is more important than you might think.'

I must have looked lost because Mr Yanagi pondered a while before offering an example. 'For instance,' he began, and I braced myself. His examples could be quite obscure. 'Do you like cheese?' he asked.

'I do.' I knew he was heading for a complicated analogy but could find no other way to respond.

'I like cheese too. Much like most people – or so I thought. A little while ago I sampled some award-winning hardcore cheese covered in mould and was blown away. This cheese was in a category all of its own, with a quite extraordinary flavour and a smell few people could tolerate. Still, a lot of people acknowledged how great it was, and it won a prize. There are those who love it and can't get enough of it. The power of taste can be pretty profound.'

I considered this as I walked along. Tuning and cheese. How on earth were the two connected?

'You see, Tomura, if a client asked you to tune their piano so it was like cheese, what would you do?'

I stopped and looked earnestly at Mr Yanagi, and raised my arms in a 'what-do-I-know?' sort of way.

'First,' he said, grabbing the bull by the horns, 'I'd find out what type of cheese they meant. 'Natural or processed, and how long it was aged for.'

Where was he going with this? And what did it have to do with finding tone?

'Bear with me.' Mr Yanagi smiled and nodded. 'Think about eggs – boiled eggs, for example. Some people like them soft-boiled, others like them harder.'

I remained nonplussed.

'But even within the soft-boiled category, there are degrees: some like the yolks to run away from them, others prefer them just on the turn – soft, but not runny. I like them a little harder myself, by the way, sprinkled with a little salt and a drizzle of olive oil. Delicious.'

I'd never eaten a boiled egg with olive oil. I didn't even own a bottle of the stuff.

Mr Yanagi continued, 'You can't say what kind of boiled egg is better. It's all a question of personal preference. Likewise, the sound the client is looking for in a piano is all a question of taste.'

Finally, he'd circled back to the point.

'To accompany steamed asparagus, an egg slow-boiled in a hot spring is the absolute best – the kind with a firm yolk but softer white. Use that almost as a sauce and it's delicious. With me so far? On the other hand, the customer may insist on it being hard-boiled at a higher temperature, and it may be because this is simply what he's used to.'

It was a little tricky to follow him exactly, but I thought I understood.

'In the same way, you have to check what standard the client is measuring against when they ask for a harder or softer sound. If they want it softer, you need to question it. Ask them what *quality* of soft sound they have in mind – is softness really what's needed in that particular case? Obviously, technique is critical, but more essential is that you're both on the same page. Ask the client to be specific about the texture of the tone they're after, and try to focus on the ideal they have in their minds.'

But even if they could pinpoint their ideal sound, that was only the beginning. Turning that concept of softness into reality was the essence of the tuner's role.

We walked on and Mr Yanagi looked up at the cloudless blue sky as though searching for something beyond it. If he was trying to find something beyond *himself*, then I too would need to extend my gaze further. But staring at the endless sky was hurting my eyes, so instead I looked back at the red berries on the yew trees along the street.

၏

THERE ARE ALL SORTS OF piano tuners and all sorts of approaches. As time passed I was more and more glad to be working under Mr Yanagi, with his floppy black hair and his eccentric metaphors, and wondered if one day I would be able to tune pianos as beautifully and effortlessly.

Some people insist that words aren't necessary. A good tone is a good tone. But rare is the client who can accurately explain what tone they're after. It's often more straight-forward simply to present them with what you are confident sounds beautiful. Most people will be happy with that.

But there are things you can interpret from their style of playing, and from what sort of music they prefer. Your choices as a tuner vary depending on the age of the pianist, the extent of their musical knowledge and level of play-ing, the characteristics of the piano itself and the shape of those characteristics, and the proportions of the room it's placed in. You weave together all of these ingredients to create the most appropriate sound.

'There are set types, you know.'

We were back in the music shop now and slap bang in the middle of one of our most earnest discussions about the essence of our work. And Mr Akino, our colleague, was taking over the conversation. He was in his early forties, thin, with silver-framed glasses, and a permanently stern look, which frightened me a little. Unusually for someone his age he had young children at home – a little girl and a newborn baby boy. Which was probably why, no matter how crowded the shop might be, no matter how busy we were, he always left exactly on time. During the day he was mostly out on house calls so I rarely saw him, had no idea how he approached tuning and what sort of sound he pro-duced. I was waiting for the chance to hear those sounds and to talk with him more about his work.

'What do you mean?' I asked Mr Akino.

'Types of clients.'

He'd often be in the office at noon, eating the bento lunch he'd brought from home. Today, he untied the gingham napkin around his bento box and held forth. 'Most people are happy as long as the piano's in tune and has a decent tone. Very few will request a specific timbre. So you have the type who has no special requests, and the type who does – there are two types, in other words.' He wiped his mouth with his paper napkin and resumed chomping.

'Do you modify the way you tune depending on which type they are?'

'Of course. There's nothing to be gained by working hard at something you haven't been asked to do.'

'So you only respond to requests when the client understands quality of tone,' I said.

It pained me to think of those types of clients the tuner considers don't understand tone – how they could end up with just a standardized, uniform type of tuning. Maybe they would come to understand quality of tone. It was possible that they would hear the sound Mr Akino created and awaken to the variety of possibilities.

If, back then on my first day of awakening, Mr Itadori had completed only a cursory tuning of the piano because it was just some rackety old grand in some school gymnasium, I wouldn't have got to where I was. I'd no doubt have been somewhere completely different, in a world without pianos.

'One more thing.' Mr Akino peered into his bento box and seemed to be checking the remaining contents. He leaned his elbows on the table for emphasis and narrowed his eyes. 'There's a pattern, too, when it comes to clients' requests. To give you an example, it's like the set vocabulary people use to describe the bouquet of a wine and its taste.'

'I'm afraid I've never drunk wine, Mr Akino.'

Mr Akino tilted his head a degree in surprise, and snorted. 'A teetotaller, are you?'

I was twenty. The only spirits I'd ever had was a sip of *omiki*, the sacred sake people had at New Year's when they made a visit to a shrine, or at autumn festivals. The training and homework on the piano-tuning course were so intense I had no time to feel in need of a drink. The first time I ever had a beer was at the welcome party when I joined this company. But the whole event had been pretty dull and I'd been left to my own devices as the new guy.

'Even if you haven't had wine you've certainly heard about these things. The fragrant nose of a certain wine, the aroma of mushrooms after rain, a smooth, velvet-like texture and so on.'

I nodded vaguely, eyeing the grains of rice that lingered at the corner of his mouth.

'There are patterns to descriptions. And tuning is similar. There are set patterns to the words we use when we talk with clients.'

'A tone with a fragrant nose and so on?'

'Yes, a bright sound, a clear sound, a lively sound – these are the sorts of requests you hear most often. To try to think what kind of sound you should make every time is too much. You set things beforehand: a bright sound means you take it to this level, a lively sound to this level, et cetera. That's all you need to do.'

'You choose a set tuning pattern to fit the set description?'

'Exactly.' Mr Akino picked up a little sausage carved into a cute octopus shape with his chopsticks. 'You go to a typical home to tune their piano. They don't ask for anything more than that, and doing anything more is pointless. In fact, if you make it too precise for them' – he popped the sausage into his mouth, and his next words were somewhat muffled – 'they might not be able to handle it.'

An offhand remark, to which I had no response. I'd heard that Mr Akino had wanted to be a concert pianist. He had graduated from a prestigious music college and had performed for a while, but had later returned to study piano tuning.

I found it discouraging to think we should aim for a piano that's merely easy to play, that anyone can handle. And that an average player would not be able to fully appreciate or benefit from a perfectly tuned piano. Was this really the case? It filled me with a sense of conflict over what I should aim for in my new life as a burgeoning piano tuner.

Nothing a Hammer Can't Fix

THE DAYS STARTED TO get shorter and cooler. By the time we left a client's house, night would already be falling.

'Sorry, but is it all right if I go straight home?' asked Mr Yanagi one evening as we walked towards the car.

'Sure,' I said. 'I'll take your case back to the office.'

'I'd appreciate it.'

A case full of tuning tools is actually quite heavy, so it was a bigger favour than it sounds.

'Actually, I've something very important to do tonight.'

'Oh, really?'

Mr Yanagi looked a little dissatisfied with my response. 'How can you be so casual about it? Wouldn't most people ask, *What's this important thing you have to attend to?*'

'Sorry. What's this important thing you have to attend to?'

'Oh, nothing!' Mr Yanagi said, before looking up, eyes smiling. 'The thing is . . .' he said, suddenly serious, 'I'm giving my girlfriend a ring.'

'Girlfriend . . . a ring . . .' I repeated awkwardly, and then, oh! 'Goo–good lu–luck!' I said, and Mr Yanagi chuckled happily.

'What are *you* getting nervous about, Tomura?'

'S–sorry.' I gave a little bow and Mr Yanagi laughed again.

'You're a quirky fellow, aren't you?'

I waved goodbye and climbed into the little white company car on my own. The edges of the twilit mountains were tinged with pink.

As I stopped at a red light a group of sixth-formers crossed in front of me. I was resting my hands on the steering wheel, gazing vacantly ahead, when I noticed one of the girls come to a halt and catch my eye. It was her! One of those twins who played the piano so amazingly. Which twin, however, I couldn't say. I nodded to her, and she stood there on the crossing and started to say something that I had to lip-read.

'You're the piano tuner, aren't you?'

I rolled down the window and poked my head out. 'I am,' I said, although I was still just an apprentice. She said something to her friend before scurrying over to the car.

'I'm so glad I bumped into you. Kazu – my older sister – said the A above middle C won't play. But the shop told her Mr Yanagi is tied up with other clients and can't come today.'

So this was the younger one, Yuni. Mr Yanagi had really appreciated their playing, but especially hers. And yet he had decided he was too busy to go to their house today. Or had Miss Kitagawa at our office, who'd probably taken the call, made excuses on his behalf?

'Would you be able to come over and check it out now?' she asked hopefully.

At that moment I wanted more than anything to help them, especially to repair a piano that wasn't playing properly. But I had to be honest. 'I'm sorry, but I doubt I'd be much help. I don't have enough technical experience.'

'So you're not a proper piano tuner yet?' She seemed disappointed.

'Well, yes. I mean, I suppose I am.'

But, you see, I'm still only – I was tempted to blurt out what I considered the truth, but managed to swallow my words. No, I *am* a tuner. This was no time for excuses.

'Then please come over and have a look at it.'

Standing there in the middle of the pedestrian crossing, she gave an energetic bow. This was definitely how she behaved, direct and full of exuberance, just like she played the piano.

'Just give me a minute.' The traffic light turned green, so I pulled over to call our office and explain. 'Is it all right if I go instead?'

'I don't see why not,' said Miss Kitagawa.

'OK, I'll be off then. I'll be in touch if I need to.'

'I'll let Mr Yanagi know. I told the client when she rang earlier that Mr Yanagi had something important on today but he would be free tomorrow.'

So it *was* Miss Kitagawa who'd blocked Kazune's request.

By the time I'd finished on the phone Yuni had left her friends and was waiting for me.

'Would you like a lift?' I asked, rolling down the left-hand window, and she hopped in beside me. 'You should sit in the back. It's safer.'

'Oh, the flat is just around the corner, so it's fine. Besides, the back seat's full of stuff.'

She was right – I had tossed both sets of our tuning tools in the back.

As she buckled herself in she turned to look at the rear seat. 'Something's fallen on the floor here.'

I wondered what it was.

'Oh, look, it's a sweet little box.'

'Hmmm?' I was concentrating on turning a corner.

'With a ribbon around it.' She sounded excited. 'It looks like a box for a ring.'

'What?!'

I was caught at another traffic light. I pulled on the handbrake and turned to get a proper look. A small box had fallen under the seat. Mr Yanagi must have dropped it. If he'd dropped the ring he was due to offer his girlfriend, what was he doing now without it? I wondered. I was worried, but cannot deny I was also a little grateful to Mr Yanagi. Yuni had been a little tense ever since she had first spotted me, but now, thanks to the ring, she seemed happy and relaxed. I reached down, retrieved the box and placed it on the dashboard. The dark red ribbon was reflected in the windscreen like a flower.

Yuni's house was close by.

'I'm back!' she called as we entered. 'And I brought the tuner with me!'

Kazune appeared from the back room. 'Great! I thought I wasn't going to be able to play the piano today. It was agony! I was beginning to wonder how I was going to sleep tonight.'

'Right,' I said, although 'agony' felt a little disproportionate here.

I stepped across the carpet to the piano and opened up the lid. Testing the keys from one end to the other, one very noticeably became stuck.

'Ah, here's your problem,' I said, my nose inches away from the strings inside.

'Can you fix it? You can fix it, can't you?' said the twins in unison, a little desperately.

I was happy to reassure them.

The flange that connected the hammer and the key had seized up. A slight adjustment and it would be back to normal.

'At this time of year you have to be careful of the humidity,' I commented.

Pianos are precise instruments made of wood. All piano tuners have it drummed into their heads to notice humidity levels, particularly in autumn and winter. If the humidity level gets too high, the wood expands. Screws loosen. Steel rusts. The tone will slip. Things are different here in Hokkaido. Humidity will still alter the sound of a piano, but what we have to be more careful of in autumn and winter is dryness. Low humidity, in other words.

'Thank you so much,' the twins said.

I pressed the key to test it, and the hammer lifted naturally. It was a simple fix.

'Could we try playing it?' Yuni asked.

'Of course.'

Yuni took her place in front of the piano. Kazune sat beside her on the other stool. Within moments they had launched into a duet.

The sound filled the room, the notes spinning and swirling. I had no idea what they were playing with such focus and energy, but the twins had come alive, the life force flowing from their dark, sparkling eyes, from their flushed cheeks, from the very ends of the hair that fell to their shoulders. They were reading from a score, but the story they told through the music was utterly their own, and in those moments it felt as if the performance they offered up was for me alone.

'Bravo!' I clapped loudly. It was an inadequate response, and I felt ashamed that it was all I could muster. 'Thank you so very much,' I added for good measure.

The girls smiled with pleasure and bowed. 'No one has ever appreciated our playing so much,' Yuni said.

'Really?' I was unsure how to respond.

'Yes, really,' Kazune confirmed.

How could that be? I wondered. That couldn't be right, at all. They were just being modest.

'It makes us glow, doesn't it?' Yuni said, nudging her sister.

'Yep.'

Yuni was holding both hands to her cheeks, while Kazune shyly scratched her head. Somehow it was now more obvious to me which twin was which.

'Well then, I'd best be off,' I said.

As I made to leave, one of the girls placed a hand on my arm. 'Wait a moment. It does feel like the whole pitch is higher. Maybe because it's so dry outside?'

'It's a little bit awkward,' both girls said at once, and I admit it slightly concerned me too. But the sound wasn't particularly off. It'd be fine without serious adjustment. If someone were to adjust it, it would need to be Mr Yanagi.

But I was so tempted to try. I could have a go, couldn't I? So the twins could enjoy the piano the way they really wanted.

I should have known.

Each piano is different, and this was my first solo tuning appointment. The room was very dry. It wasn't hot but still I was sweating. I shouldn't have been nervous, but my fingers were trembling. I should have turned the pins slightly but I overdid it. I tried to turn them back, and my fingers slipped. Something I usually found so simple was taking for ever. *Just a touch, just a touch*, I thought, but found the sounds shifting in directions I didn't want them to go. The tone became totally uneven. The more I fussed over it, the worse it got, and the more flustered I became, the further the vibrations of sound slipped out of control. Time passed and I was covered in sweat. Everything I'd learned, all the nights of practice I'd put in at the showroom, flew right out of the window.

My mobile buzzed in my breast pocket. Stepping away from the piano, I looked at the display. It was from Mr Yanagi. The one person I hoped wouldn't call, but also the one I hoped *would* call.

'It's me. Sorry to bother you, but the ring—'

'I have it,' I said in a flash.

'Oh, what a relief! I was in a panic about it.' After a pause he said, 'What's wrong, Tomura? Is everything OK?'

It must have been in my voice. I gave up trying to hide it. 'I'm so sorry, Mr Yanagi, but you need to attend an urgent tuning appointment, first thing tomorrow morning.' It had taken all my strength of will to say this, and I also bowed to Mr Yanagi on the other end of the line. 'I'm here checking the piano at the Sakuras' place, but I think I've really messed it up.'

Mr Yanagi was silent. 'O–kay,' he finally said slowly.

I felt completely dreadful at my own foolishness and ambition. I'd plunged ahead on my own, had screwed up, and tomorrow we would need to return free of charge.

'But hang on,' said one of the twins. They were in the corner of the room, quietly watching me. Yuni, I think it was, strode briskly over to the piano. 'This is actually a really great sound.' She struck the A above middle C. It rang out clear, free and relaxed, far from the agitation I felt. 'And this sound is good, too, to go along with it.' She tapped the adjacent key. *Plonk, plonk.* The one next to that. And next to that.

'It might sound a little bold, but I totally get what you're going for. A commanding sound. I think that's the sound I was after. So even if it isn't exactly what you had in mind, I don't dislike it at all. It just needs a little more – a little more *something*.'

'Totally,' Kazune chimed in. 'No matter how well it all goes together, if it's tuned to a totally harmonious, flawless sound, that's sort of disappointing, even bland. I prefer this sort of defiant sound, too.'

Defiant? What was I trying to defy? All I could do was remain silent. I wasn't defying anything. I'd simply bitten off more than I could chew.

'I'm really sorry.' As I bowed my head, I felt hot tears begin to fill my eyes. 'Tomorrow morning Mr Yanagi will come over. Again, I'm so sorry.'

'It's OK – *we're* the ones who dragged you over here!' Yuni said.

I apologized once more and left the room. My briefcase felt unduly heavy. I'd totally blown it, I thought. Complain about Mr Akino's methods? Who was *I* to do *that*?

I left their apartment building and walked slowly to the car park. It was dark now and the temperature had dropped. The windscreen had fogged up so I drove back carefully, while other drivers beeped at me to speed up.

Back at the shop the shutters were closed on the ground floor but lights were still on upstairs. It wasn't so late, but on days when there were no piano lessons the shop closed at six thirty. I hoped no one else was lingering after hours.

I walked in through the service entrance and trudged upstairs, the two cases weighing me down. Expecting no one else to be there, I opened the door and found that, today of all days, Mr Itadori was still around. He had on one of the jackets he wore on visits, so I assumed he'd just returned from a client. I couldn't look him in the face; there was so much I wanted to learn from him, but I felt so hopeless. More than ever I felt there was probably nothing Mr Itadori could teach someone like me.

'Good evening, Tomura,' he said, looking up from some papers.

I responded in a weak mumble; I seemed incapable of holding it together.

'Is something wrong?'

'Mr Itadori.' I tried to keep my voice from shaking. 'What should I do to be good at tuning?'

I realized immediately what a stupid question it was. I was nowhere near good – I couldn't even master the basics. The rule was to spend six months shadowing a more experienced tuner and learning from him, but I'd broken that. I recalled the legend of Orpheus who'd looked behind him at the last moment, sending his dead wife back to the underworld. Had he really been just a few steps from the world of the living?

'An excellent question, Tomura,' Mr Itadori said gravely. He looked as though he was pondering this deeply.

The original sound he had produced so long ago in the school gym suddenly floated into my memory. The first piano sounds I'd ever heard. I was still searching to hear them again, but I hadn't come any closer. Maybe I'd never be able to. I trembled with a sort of fear – the kind you feel when you first set foot into a dense forest.

'What should I do?' I said.

To which Mr Itadori replied, 'If you don't mind?' He held out a tuning hammer. 'Do you fancy using this?'

I grasped the handle. It was heavier than expected but fitted my hand perfectly.

'A gift.'

I was taken aback and must have looked doubtful.

'Don't you need it?' he asked.

'Oh yes! I really *do*,' I replied. The forest might be deep but I knew in that moment I had no plans to turn back. 'It looks really easy to use.'

'It doesn't just look easy to use – it *does* actually make the whole job easier. If you'd like it, it's yours. To celebrate,' Mr Itadori said serenely, his eyes suddenly twinkling.

'Celebrate what?'

On this of all days. The worst day of my life.

'Somehow I get the feeling from watching you, Tomura, that you're on your way now. So I thought this was a moment worth celebrating.'

'Thank you very much.' My lips quivered. Mr Itadori was trying to encourage me. I was standing at the entrance to the forest and here he was telling me I was on the right path.

So many times I'd watched furtively as he cleaned the tuning hammers, longing to hold one, desperate to learn more about the tools he used and how best to handle them. I never imagined I'd get to have one of my very own so soon.

'Mr Itadori, can I ask you a question?' I clasped the tuning hammer tightly in my right hand. 'What sort of sound do you aim for when you tune?'

The question I'd been holding in for so long.

'The sound I aim for?' he asked, relaxed as ever, leaning back in his seat, arms behind his head.

I hoped that, as far as possible, his answer would be neither too specific nor unattainable.

'Tomura, are you familiar with Tamiki Hara?'

I'd heard the name. I didn't think he was a piano tuner. Was he a concert pianist?

'This is the way he put it.' Mr Itadori cleared his throat and sat up. 'Bright, quiet, crystal-clear writing that evokes fond memories, that seems a touch sentimental yet is unsparing and deep, writing as lovely as a dream, yet as exact as reality.'

I wasn't sure what he meant, but then it hit me. Tamiki Hara was a novelist. A name I'd learned at school in Japanese literature lessons.

'Tamiki Hara wrote that he was enraptured by this kind of writing, and when I first read his words I was carried away. I felt that this exactly described the ideal sound I was hoping for.'

He'd substituted sound for writing.

'I'm sorry, but could you say that all again?' I said, taking a seat.

I wanted to listen extra carefully the second time around.

'One more time, that's all,' Mr Itadori said, stretching his arms above his head, pulling at his brown suede jacket – a garment that had seen much better days. He cleared his throat again. 'Bright, quiet, crystal-clear writing that evokes fond memories, that seems a touch sentimental yet is unsparing and deep, writing as lovely as a dream, yet as exact as reality.'

That's precisely the sound Mr Itadori produced – the sound that changed my world for ever. It had taken four years and now I was finally here. I was compelled to forge ahead. It was the only way open to me.

'Oh.' Mr Itadori looked over as the door suddenly opened. A second later Mr Yanagi bustled in.

'Mr Yanagi!' I said.

He strode over, anger in his eyes, instead of his normal friendly twinkle. He grabbed hold of the tuning case I'd brought in earlier. 'Let's go.'

Go where? I almost asked. But I knew. I hurriedly took hold of my own case. I was about to say, 'But, Mr Yanagi, you had something very important to do today.'

Before I could get this out, he said, 'I came to fetch the ring. I'll go back to my girlfriend later. But first, let's do what needs to be done as efficiently as we can.'

It wasn't something that could be dealt with quickly, and Mr Yanagi was well aware of that.

'I'm really sorry about all this,' I said, a little meekly.

'Everyone blows it the first time. It can't be helped. You were just a little too hasty, Tomura.' Mr Yanagi now turned to Mr Itadori, who sat listening, hands in pockets, a bemused look on his face. 'Have a nice evening,' Mr Yanagi said with a grunt.

My bag in my right hand, my own new tuning hammer in my left, I trotted off after Mr Yanagi. I turned around to say goodbye to Mr Itadori and saw he'd unbuttoned his brown jacket, rolled up his sleeves and was diligently polishing his tuning tools.

Good Sheep Make for
a Good Sound

THE NEEDLE THRUST THROUGH a felt hammer, once, twice. Very deliberately, and without hesitation, Mr Yanagi pierced the felt one more time, then deftly returned the hammer to its original position. He moved on to the next hammer. Once, twice, three times. Standing beside him I kept a careful count of how many times he did this, before realizing that the number wasn't important. Rather, it was the placement of the needle, the direction, the precise angle, the depth – something you could only grasp by instinct and feel.

Today's client, an elderly lady, wanted us to retune an equally aged piano. She was apologetic: the piano clearly hadn't been looked after, although the casing had been nicely dusted and polished and looked rather lovely in the tranquil old room filled with antiques. It was an upright model by a Japanese manufacturer no longer in business and it had lingered unplayed and untuned for years.

'Do you think you can get this piano back to the way it was?' the lady asked us.

'We'll do everything we can,' Mr Yanagi reassured her, although given the instrument's state of neglect, it might require extensive repairs as well.

The client seemed satisfied with Mr Yanagi's reply. She inserted a brass key into the lock and turned it with a click.

The keyboard was ivory, a little yellowed with time. Mr Yanagi pressed a few keys to test them. The sound was muffled and certainly out of tune, but not as bad as I'd imagined. He played two octaves with both hands, then as the lady patiently watched from the corner of the room, he quickly twisted the screws, lifted off the front panel and placed it on the hard floor. He examined the strings and hammers, and turned to her with a broad smile.

'You asked if we could return it to its original condition?' he said quietly. 'Well, I think we can. And with a little further adjustment, I think we can achieve an even better sound than it had originally.'

He added, 'Of course this is up to you. We can either bring back its original sound, or else try to achieve a different tone that you'd prefer now.'

The lady touched her whitish hair as she considered. 'Either option is OK?' she asked hesitantly. 'You really can do either?'

'Absolutely, either one. We'll aim to create the tone you find most pleasing.'

With this assurance from Mr Yanagi, the lady smiled broadly, looking relieved. 'All right, then please tune it to the way it used to sound.'

'Of course,' Mr Yanagi replied. Then, as if the question had just struck him, he said, 'May I ask who used to play this piano?'

'My daughter. She gave up before she became really good. Neither my husband nor I play, so maybe it was inevitable.'

In a quiet voice she continued, 'We didn't look after the piano in the days when my daughter used to play. It probably didn't show itself at its best. I feel bad asking for it to be returned to its original sound if, as you say, you can make it sound even better.'

'No, please don't feel that way,' I said, shaking my head. 'Every person has their own preferred sound.'

She looked somewhat comforted at this, but it was true. I understood why she wanted to get back to the way it sounded when her daughter had played.

'It'll probably take us two or three hours. We'll just go ahead, so please don't worry about us. I'll let you know if I have any questions.' Mr Yanagi nodded to her and I bowed.

After the lady had shuffled silently out of the room, Mr Yanagi set to work. Improving the timbre of the piano required adjustment of the voicing as well as the tuning.

First he removed all the hammers, along with the wooden frame. The hammers of a piano are made of densely compacted woollen felt and should be neither too hard nor too soft in texture. Too hard and they produce a tinny tinkling sound; too soft and the sound is stifled. The final step in adjusting the voicing is to rub the hammers down with a fine file or adjust their elasticity by piercing them with a needle.

It's a very precise operation and hard to get absolutely right. There are certain spots to file down or pierce, and you only learn these by feel. You file down or pierce with a needle, concentrating on the type of sound you're aiming for – and each and every piano, each and every hammer, is different. It's a laborious and time-consuming process. If your hand slips, you can ruin a hammer. It's tense work, but as I watched Mr Yanagi's deftness of touch, it looked enjoyable too. Satisfying. How wonderful it would be to create a sound like this myself one day. To discover the unique personality of a piano, take into consideration the individual qualities of the pianist, determine the sound they prefer, and then create that very sound.

The voicing Mr Yanagi found in the instrument was enchanting. Never one for gaudiness or show, he came up with a light and delicate tone.

'Oh, how delightful that sounds!' The tuning was finished, and the lady smiled sweetly at what she heard. 'It's perfect – look, the whole room is bright and cheery again.'

I was happy to see the old lady so pleased, even though I could take none of the credit. It's a pure kind of happiness that a successful tuning brings – for the tuner as well as the client – not unlike the joy to be found in seeing wildflowers along the roadside in bloom.

'You used the needle a lot, didn't you?' I asked this in the car on the way back to the shop. Mr Yanagi seemed a little exhausted, and had slumped down in his seat. 'Is it because it hadn't been tuned for so long?'

I knew I shouldn't question him when he looked so weary, but I couldn't help myself. I wished I could take notes, but of course had to keep my hands on the wheel, since I was always the one driving. There was so very much I needed to learn from Mr Yanagi.

'You used the needle to get it back to the sound it had originally, I assume? What I mean is, were there lots of places in the hammers where they'd been pierced before? Even if you can't see them, can you tell by touch?'

'Nope,' muttered Mr Yanagi, as he sprawled against the seat. 'Those hammer heads had never been pierced before. They were old, but like new. The previous tuner was not the type who'd pierce them.'

'What?'

Opinion is divided among tuners on the matter of whether or not to pierce the hammers. With brand-new hammers that are a little tinny in sound, piercing them gives a soft and richer tone. But if you don't pierce them in exactly the right spot it makes them deteriorate more quickly. It's both a time-consuming and risky business, so many tuners choose never to pierce the hammers.

'Then why did you pierce those hammers so much?'

'Because I knew that would produce a good tone.'

I glanced at him in surprise, but he went on casually, eyes closed. 'It was a shame to let that piano rot away. It needs to be played.'

'But doesn't that mean you ended up producing something different from how it originally sounded?'

'If you compare the preferred tone from those days and now, they would be different, I expect.'

But the client had chosen to get it back to its *original condition*.

'The idea of original sound is the issue. Isn't it more important that a person's memories are evoked, rather than the exact same effect created? The happy memories of when her daughter was little and played that piano.'

I remained a little confused.

'What that lady really wants is not a faithful reproduction of the way that piano sounded, but rather to bring back her memories. Either way, the original sound doesn't exist any longer. So I decided it was best to bring out the tunefulness which that particular piano was originally designed to create. If a sweet sound floats into the air, then the memories will follow.'

I didn't know what to say, had no idea if that had been the right decision. What would I have done in his place? I would probably have kept strictly to what I'd been told to do and tried to recapture the original sound. But it struck me then that valuing that goal above all else might mean missing the opportunity to create a richer, fuller tone. The thought alone was painful to me.

And that's the crux of it: it's very limiting and stressful to work solely within the scope of what the client thinks they are after. The true pleasures of working as a tuner lie beyond that, beyond the simple embodiment of the client's own mental conception of how the piano should sound.

'Those were wonderful hammers,' said Mr Yanagi, waking up now with a yawn and appearing more cheerful.

'I thought so too. They should have been harder, but they still had that feel of wool to them.'

Hammers made from sheep's wool, striking strings of steel. And that becomes music. Those white hammers that Mr Yanagi had pierced – small and old though they might be – fulfilled an extraordinary and wonderful purpose.

'I heard that in one of the countries in the Middle East sheep are a symbol of wealth.'

Mr Yanagi cradled his fingers behind his head. 'That just means that the wealthy can afford to have lots of sheep, doesn't it?'

'Yep.'

Having been raised next to a sheep farm, a part of me thought of livestock purely in terms of monetary value. But what came to mind in that moment, thinking of sheep, was a scene of those serene animals in a green, open pasture, chewing lazily on their grass. Good sheep make for a good sound – to me that felt like a richness in itself. But there are people who picture wealth more in terms of a city packed with high-rise buildings.

Kazune Is Extraordinary

THE TWINS WOULD ON occasion stop by the shop on their way home from school. Sometimes together, sometimes individually. They'd come and peruse sheet music, or piano books in our book corner.

Ever since I'd messed up trying to tune their piano they seemed to feel closer to me. They'd stop by for no particular reason to say hello, chat about the piano or trivial things that had happened at school, then flash me a smile and leave, apologizing for having bothered me at work.

Miss Kitagawa thought it adorable how the girls would always bob their heads at the same time in a little bow. 'That's one perk of being a tuner for a home with girls in the sixth form.'

Actually Mr Yanagi was their tuner. I just tagged along. And besides, I was the one who'd botched the tuning.

Today, unusually, I was called downstairs by the receptionist and found one of the twins awaiting me – I couldn't tell which – a solemn look on her face. When she saw me she bowed.

'Hello. Sorry to bother you at work.'

'No problem.'

It was Kazune. Kazune was the one who always looked this serious.

'I'm really sorry,' she said suddenly, and bowed again. 'I'm really sorry to always impose on you.'

'No, it's absolutely fine! No trouble at all. What's up?'

Kazune's lips tightened. 'I thought maybe I could talk to you about something, Mr Tomura. I'm sorry.' Apologizing once more, she continued, 'There's a recital on soon.'

'I see.'

'Didn't Yuni mention it?'

Yuni had dropped by a few days earlier but hadn't said anything.

Kazune lowered her gaze when she saw me shake my head. 'She's always been like that. Nothing ever fazes her, and she never gets nervous before a recital. She thinks if she enjoys playing that's enough, and it's true that when she plays freely in that way, her performance is really wonderful. On days when she doesn't feel like practising, she simply doesn't. I could never do that. I end up practising whatever mood I'm in.'

'That's pretty extraordinary.'

'Yup, that's Yuni,' she said, nodding.

'Actually, I think *you're* amazing, Kazune,' I said, and I really meant it.

'No, I'm not,' she shot back.

Was practising something you should do in spite of yourself? I didn't play, so I couldn't say. But if you really did end up practising even when you weren't in the mood, I'd call that pretty amazing.

'I just like practising on the keyboard,' she went on. 'When a new piece turns out well, it makes me feel so good inside. And when I play at home my family and my piano teacher always praise me.'

Kazune said this quite deadpan. It didn't sound as though she was being arrogant. *They praise me, but what does that matter?* is how Kazune probably felt. And that was the right attitude. Garnering praise shouldn't be the main goal when you play the piano.

'But when it comes down to the actual recital, it's always Yuni. She's the one who gives a stellar performance – even though I sound better when I practise. In recitals or even in a small competition Yuni's the one who always gets the rapturous applause.'

I could understand that. Yuni's playing was clear as a bell, and I always felt moved by it.

It made me think about my brother, two years younger than me. Whenever we played our special chess game, *shogi*, at home I was better, but when we competed in contests in town he always beat me. It wasn't as though he was holding back when we played at home. There are just people who are stronger in their play when it really counts, or who are consistently lucky in competitions.

'Does that mean you make mistakes when you perform?'

'No, not at all.' Kazune made that point clear. 'But Yuni takes it to another level. She completely sparkles in front of an audience. There's a brilliance to her. When the time comes, she really shines, really captivates people.'

'That's OK, isn't it? You can't show what you're really capable of in front of an audience, so you let Yuni take the prize. You play in your own way and for your own reasons. What's wrong with that?'

Kazune looked at me, wide-eyed. 'You're right.' Her lips slowly curled up in a smile. 'I don't exactly fall apart when I play to an audience, so I shouldn't worry about it, should I?'

In actual fact, I remember resenting my own younger sibling. I envied him every time he snatched away the prize that I felt should have been mine, but I pretended not to care.

'I've been wasting your time worrying about pointless stuff – like it's all a question of luck or something you're born with. I don't want to lose sight of more important things. Sorry to have bothered you,' Kazune said. She bowed twice to me and then left the shop with a small wave, the doorbell jangling behind her.

I was left hoping that she wouldn't end up feeling resentful towards Yuni. It's a lot more painful to be jealous of someone than to be the object of jealousy.

I was about to take the stairs up to the office when Mr Yanagi caught up with me. He was a little breathless and looked as though he'd just arrived.

'Well, that was a surprise. Wasn't that Kazune-*chan*?'

He sounded in a good mood.

'You can tell the twins apart, can't you, Mr Yanagi?'

Tuning case still in his hand, Mr Yanagi inclined his head, a questioning look on his face. 'What do you mean, Tomura?'

'Makes sense as you've been going to their house since they were little.'

'Tomura, how old do you think I am, anyway? When the twins were young, so was I.'

'Oh!'

There was a three- or four-year age difference between the twins and me, and I guessed there must be ten years at least between them and Mr Yanagi. I was wondering how old the twins had been when he first started tuning their piano, when he suddenly said, 'Their uniforms are slightly different.'

'Uniforms?'

'Even if you can't tell their faces apart, anybody can figure it out by looking at their uniforms.' He began to sound impatient. 'Are you telling me you haven't noticed?'

'Ah well – now that you mention it.'

Mr Yanagi broke into a grin.

Now that he'd said it, I realized their uniforms were indeed different. Kazune had told me once that they were attending different sixth-form colleges since Yuni had better grades.

'No, it's because all Kazune can think of is the piano,' Yuni had said on another occasion, laughing. 'Our grades are about the same, though I do better in maths. For me, once I've psyched out the first problem, then I feel I can do the next one too. But Kazune doesn't feel excited about anything except the piano.'

Identical twins don't just look alike but should share all the same genes, so it's hard to say where a small discrepancy might show. I suppose differences in whether they're good with numbers or not, what school they attend and what sort of friends they make there might emerge over time. And in the way they play the piano, of course.

'You give it your all with the twins, yet don't spot that they wear different uniforms? What's that about?'

It wasn't that I gave it my all. I just loved the way they played.

'I'm looking forward to seeing how the twins develop,' he said finally.

II

BEGINNER'S LEVEL
AT BEST

Close Your Eyes and Decide

I WAS ABOUT TO BEGIN my second year with the company. No new employees had been hired, so as before I remained low down in the pecking order. Still, it was a relief. I had no idea how I'd cope if they hired a younger employee who was more talented than me. The fact was that I believed any new employee would be better than me. It still took a long time for me to get a piano in tune. More worryingly, although I could more or less get it in tune, I couldn't go beyond that. I struggled desperately with the most critical aspect of tuning – deciding on timbre and tone.

'Close your eyes and decide,' Mr Yanagi advised me one day during one of our chats in the shop.

I couldn't get it. 'Wait, you're saying just go for it?'

'No, that isn't what I mean. Closing your eyes doesn't mean you're getting desperate.

'For instance,' he explained kindly, 'a chef gets quite serious when it comes to tasting a dish. He takes a deep breath, closes his eyes and makes an immediate decision as to how it should taste. Tuners, too, need to be decisive about the sound or they'll end up dithering.'

I was writing this all down – *Close your eyes* – in my notebook. Mr Yanagi added quickly, 'Some people don't actually close their eyes. I don't close mine.'

'Then who does?'

'I don't know. By closing your eyes I just mean that you have to listen carefully and decide on a tone. It's a kind of metaphor, I suppose.'

Meta, I added in my notebook. Mr Yanagi used so many metaphors when he talked: cheese, wine and so on. If closing your eyes was yet another metaphor, then what was I supposed to take literally?

Mr Yanagi stood up. He was scheduled to tune the pianos in a number of rural schools. It was a large area we had to cover; some jobs were two hours away by car. Since it was such a distance, he would often stop off at kindergartens and local community centres to tune their pianos along the way, too. It added up to a long and gruelling day.

'I'll be at a home appointment today,' I said. 'I'll close my eyes and do my best.'

'You know, some day I'm going to pass all the schools over to you, Tomura.'

I wasn't ready yet, but I looked forward to the day I could help at these places where children would be encountering a piano in the music room or gym for the first time.

My schedule now involved tuning pianos in homes a few times a week. In cases where the piano hadn't been tuned in years, or there seemed to be some problem with it, Mr Yanagi took the lead, and I just watched and learned. I wasn't ready for that responsibility yet, and while I felt apologetic towards my older colleagues that I hadn't made faster progress, frankly it was also a relief. There is nothing more pitiable than a piano tuned by an incompetent technician.

I was just preparing to leave for a job when my phone extension rang.

It was a call from Miss Kitagawa.

'Your first appointment this morning – Mr Watanabe – needs to cancel. He wants to reschedule for next week at the same time.'

'All right. That'll work.'

I hung up the phone and noted the appointment on my desk calendar, crossing out the one for today.

'Was that a cancellation?' Mr Yanagi was almost out of the door but turned around before leaving. 'An appointment for this morning just cancelled?'

Tunings are usually carried out just once a year. Normally a tuning for a home piano takes two hours and is by appointment only, but clients often change the appointment or fail to keep it. Perhaps they find it a burden to have someone come to their house and stay for two hours, which I can sort of understand. But changing an appointment so casually seemed proof at the time of how little some people really cared for their pianos, and the whole thing left me feeling quite deflated.

All we need is a piano. The client doesn't need to be by our side the whole time, and the ordinary household noises they might make – vacuuming or using the washing machine – don't bother us in the least.

'Some clients even think they can't cook while we're tuning,' Mr Yanagi said.

'Can't cook? Why not?'

'They're convinced that the smell would interfere with our sense of hearing.'

'I see.' I could sort of picture that.

'It's best to let the client know in advance that they can carry on as usual, to make things a little easier for them. Truthfully, though, if their phone rings, that can mess with the hertz as we tune.'

'Don't they often also change their appointment because they haven't cleaned the room yet?' Miss Kitagawa had left her desk and come over to join us.

'We don't care if they clean up or not, we just want them to stop postponing their appointments, don't we?!'

Dirty rooms don't bother us, although one home we'd visited the week before had so much stuff scattered all over the floor we had trouble finding a spot to lay down the panels and parts we'd removed. It was also a shock to discover how the clothes flung all over the floor absorbed the sound and completely altered the way the piano resonated.

Mr Yanagi saw I was stuck for a response and laughed. 'Tomura loves things to be all neat and tidy.'

As we stood there chatting, Mr Itadori happened by, carrying a case in his arms.

'Somebody cancelled on you?'

'Yes.'

'If you have time, would you like to come along with me?'

I couldn't believe my ears, because Mr Itadori was scheduled to tune at a concert hall today.

'Su–sure,' I managed to stutter.

'We're leaving soon.'

A German pianist – a virtuoso, a keyboard magician, people called him – was touring Japan. And I had heard that Mr Itadori was to tune the piano for the recital the following day. The pianist was giving only a handful of performances in Japan, and I had no idea why he'd give one here in this little northern town so far off the beaten track, although I was certainly looking forward to it. I'd be able to hear – live – the sound I'd listened to so many times on CD. It was the first time in my life I'd ever bought a ticket to a concert.

Hurriedly, I got my things together. I figured I wouldn't need my tuning tools. But maybe I should bring them? No, they'd only get in the way. But wait – going empty-handed wasn't good. Maybe I should take them, just in case? *No, no, that's no good either. Oh, maybe I should offer to carry Mr Itadori's bag for him? And I'll need a pen and pad to take notes.*

It seemed that Mr Akino, whom I hadn't seen in a while and was now seated at the desk across from me, had said something. Without looking up he said, 'Sounds like congratulations are in order.'

His face didn't appear stern at all, as it often was. He wore a gentle expression, the kind that convinced you that something auspicious had taken place, but his tone was as sharp as always.

At first he'd been rather reserved in his dealings with me, perhaps because we'd had few opportunities to interact. As he got used to me, he relaxed and spoke his mind more freely. When he did so, his words struck me deeply, and I remembered them and carried them with me.

Congratulations. That was right on the mark. All I could manage was to carry Mr Itadori's bag, but I was awestruck simply at being able to accompany him on a tuning job.

I had decided not to be fazed by it, though. That would be to waste the opportunity. And this was an amazing opportunity – to watch Mr Itadori tune a piano for a world-class pianist.

I went over to the office whiteboard and wrote in the name of the concert hall in the column next to my name.

'So why are you going, Tomura? What use will you be?'

Mr Akino was scoffing now, and this took me by surprise. Everywhere you go there are unpleasant people who take pleasure in running roughshod over others' feelings. Be it in a small village in the mountains, in a college in town, among our clients, even in our office, it makes no difference. I tried to convince myself that worrying about it wasn't going to get me anywhere. But he did, after all, have a point. And because he was right, I had to respond.

'In five years,' I began, then corrected myself. 'I'm sorry – in *ten* years. I'll study hard so that ten years from now it'll bear fruit.'

'Even if you study . . . and even in ten years . . .' Mr Akino snorted dismissively. I decided to ignore his contempt, and walked out of the door.

∽

THERE WAS A SHIFT IN the air the moment we entered the spacious auditorium of the concert hall. Suddenly I found myself sensing the vastness of the forest – that selfsame forest all over again. All the commotion outside was forgotten.

With permission from the venue manager, we sat in the middle of the hall to get the clearest view possible of the stage and the piano.

'It's a really good idea,' Mr Itadori said, nodding, 'to check how the piano appears from the point of view of the audience. You have to strip away your own preconceptions.'

From our seats in the auditorium we were presented with the tableau of the piano on one side of the unlit stage. Even in its stillness, it was beautiful.

'I'll go around through the dressing room, and you can come up from here,' Mr Itadori said, asking me to seek permission from the manager first.

The still air, the controlled humidity and temperature, the wooden baffles lining the walls and ceiling – I wondered what the acoustics would be like in here. Slowly I approached the stage and, without taking my eyes off the grand piano, walked around to the side and up the steps, where Mr Itadori was already heaving up the lid, his tuning tools laid out on the floor.

With both hands, he played an octave. The piano, part of the scenery until now, began to breathe. As each note was struck, the piano raised its heavy body and stretched its folded arms and legs, preparing to break into song, about to spread its wings. This was unlike any piano I'd ever seen. I pictured an enormous lion, slowly rising, eyes on its prey.

A concert-hall piano was a creature unlike any other, the sound so different from what I'd heard from the pianos in people's homes. As unlike as morning and night, pencil and ink.

My palms were damp and I felt utterly overwhelmed. Getting a small personal piano in top condition and tuning a concert grand such as this – the two operations were poles apart. All I could do was stand there in awe.

Mr Itadori pressed each key repeatedly, paused, then pressed again, listening intently to the quality of the sounds as he manipulated his tuning hammer.

Something was approaching. What it was I couldn't say. My heart was pounding. I had the premonition that something immense was drawing near. I could see gently sloping mountains. The scenery from the house I was born and raised in. The mountains I had never really given much thought to, nor ever stopped to look at much. But I now recalled how they would look strangely vibrant and alive the morning after a storm. And I realized that what I'd taken simply as mountains included so very much more: soil and trees, flowing water, grass growing, the blowing of the wind, animals of all kinds. One spot in the distance came into sharp focus. A single tree growing on the mountainside, its green leaves rustling.

And so it was with the sound of the piano: the instant Mr Itadori tuned it, what had been merely an indistinct tone now became lustrous, lingering and vibrant. Single notes now began to leap ahead, entwining with the others, taking on depth in tone and timbre. From a leaf to a tree, from a tree to a forest, to the very mountains themselves. Soon it would transform into music.

In that moment, I sensed I had been a lost child, wandering aimlessly in search of a purpose. Call it a purpose or a sign, a landmark or a feeling. I knew this was the sound I'd been seeking. As long as I had this sound, I could live – this was all I could be sure of. I recalled myself ten years earlier, how I'd felt free in the forest. Incomplete, not yet liberated from the constraints of the body, but still utterly free. The gods of my world then were the trees, the leaves, the berries, the soil. But now it was sound that guided me.

By the time I exited the concert hall it was already getting dark. In preparation for tomorrow's recital Mr Itadori was also heading home. Tomorrow he'd meet up with the pianist for final adjustments and the rehearsal. For the actual performance, he would remain backstage to watch over the piano. He'd be hard at work the entire day.

The two of us walked to the car park in companionable silence. I couldn't think of anything to say. I felt quietly exhilarated, but at the same time calm and collected.

Fastening my seatbelt in the car, I was finally able to speak. 'That was amazing.'

Mr Itadori turned to me and smiled. 'I'm very pleased to hear you say that.'

A pause and then I asked, 'Mr Itadori, why did you hire me?'

It was the managing director who had the final say on hiring decisions, so I knew Mr Itadori couldn't have been entirely responsible. Still, I suspected it was through his good offices that the Eto Music Shop had taken me on.

'First come, first served,' he said.

'By first you mean—'

'Whoever gets there soonest. That's the way we've always done it.'

'Oh.'

So they didn't hire me because of my abilities or prospects.

'It's important never to give up,' said Mr Itadori simply.

Give up at what? I wanted to ask, but swallowed back the question. I wasn't going to give up. But I knew full well that not giving up didn't necessarily mean you would succeed.

Mr Itadori didn't add any more. He just sat there in the passenger seat, quietly staring ahead. I kept quiet, too, and started the car.

I felt I'd given up on quite a lot in my life. Born and raised in a remote mountain village, my family barely scraped by. The benefits that children in towns took for granted rarely came our way, and there were all kinds of things I had to forgo.

But I didn't find that particularly painful. It doesn't hurt so much to lose out on things if you never hoped for them in the first place. What really hurts is having things right there in front of you, and wanting them, and not being able to reach them.

I had given up on art, for example – or more specifically, on paintings. I simply didn't understand them. At primary school, up in the mountains, there was a field trip once a year, when we were taken by bus to an art museum in a big city. They called it the Art Appreciation Outing. But even if I looked at the exhibited paintings, and thought, *Isn't that beautiful, isn't that interesting*, it never went further than that. Beyond finding some paintings beautiful, I couldn't grasp what might be special about them.

But maybe that was OK, after all. Simply to know what you like and not worry about why. If it made you feel good, perhaps that was enough. So I decided to stop stifling myself with such thoughts as *I don't understand art*, or *That's not the way to appreciate it*.

And then, at the age of seventeen, I heard that piano in the gymnasium, and for the first time I felt like shouting aloud. Unconsciously, that's what I'd been seeking – that instant, unambiguous emotional response.

～

BACK IN THE CAR WITH Mr Itadori, I muttered, 'I don't think I'll give up.' There was no reason to give up. I could see clearly what was needed and what wasn't.

Mr Akino was there when I got back to the office. 'So how was it?' He seemed genuinely interested rather than looking for a chance to pour scorn.

Thoughts had whirled around in my head as I watched Mr Itadori tune but I didn't mention any of those. If this man was going to have a retort for everything I said, I decided to keep it short and simple.

'I thought the pianist and the audience must be exceedingly lucky to hear that piano in concert.'

For a second Mr Akino's dark eyes widened behind his glasses. 'Really?' he said. 'So how did he handle the voicing?'

'I don't know the details,' I answered honestly. 'But it was the first time I saw in practice that changing the direction of the piano legs could adjust the projection of sound so profoundly.'

In tuning school we'd been taught that changing the direction of the brass casters on the bottom of the legs alters the piano's centre of gravity. Mr Itadori showed me how this works in a way that was easy to follow. If you place your hands wider than your shoulders when you do push-ups it changes how you have to apply your strength, putting more pressure on your core. With the piano, moving the casters adds more power to the soundboard. Using this concise analogy of push-ups, Mr Itadori explained that as he moved the direction of the casters it would be like lifting the entire baseplate of the piano with his back. This alone was enough to alter the resonance dramatically.

'Well, aren't *you* the star pupil?' Mr Akino's voice was dripping with sarcasm. 'You're way too simplistic about things. That's not the essence of Mr Itadori's tuning, not at all. Were you half asleep or something? You're too spoiled. And Mr Itadori treats you with kid gloves. He shows you every tiny thing he does, doesn't he? By doing that isn't he in fact looking down on you?'

'Of course not. I'm still learning,' I said and ended the conversation.

Make Your Craft Invisible

THE FOLLOWING DAY I accompanied Mr Yanagi on a tuning job and brought up what Mr Akino had said.

'Ah, Mr Akino . . . Don't let it bother you.'

As he paced along, pulling his tuning bag behind him on wheels for a change, I saw that he was smiling. I knew then that he didn't think badly of Mr Akino.

'He annoyed me at first, too,' he continued. 'Not to mention his claims that your average client is happy so long as you adjust things so they're *boom-snap*.'

'What?' I asked, and Mr Yanagi grinned.

'That sort of sound was popular with stereos for a time. A really booming bass at the lower end with a snappy, crisp sound in the higher registers. Tweak a piano so it sounded like that and people thought it was good.'

I imagined Mr Akino was teasing him to an extent. Popularity was a factor we had to consider, and part of the tuner's job was, after all, to adjust it to a tone the clients found pleasing.

'I thought he shouldn't say such stupid things.' He spoke quickly as we walked through the car park. 'I thought he was making fun of tuning and of our clients. I thought he'd just not come across any discerning clients and I felt sorry for him. Nonetheless . . .' He glanced over at me as though an interesting new idea had just come to him. 'Tomura, why don't you try to ask Mr Akino to take you out on a job sometime?' He didn't miss the wry look on my face. 'That *boom-snap* talk is just that – talk. Actually, he does a really good job. Despite the spiky attitude and the things he says.'

'Seriously?'

Mr Yanagi nodded. 'I don't know if he's conscious of it or not, but he never cuts corners. He looks like he doesn't care, but he does a good job. He loves and respects the piano. Though I bet he'd deny it if you asked him.'

Even if I were to ask Mr Akino to let me tag along, I doubted he'd agree. And I couldn't say I wanted to, either. I felt as though I was drowning in things I didn't understand and wasn't ready for, desperate to get purchase on the cliff face.

I finished work on time and headed over to the concert hall. It had a different feel to it today. Yesterday it had worn the hushed air of a forest in the evening. Tonight, full of the bustle of the crowds, it reminded me of a forest in summer, alive and lush with greenery.

The audience was considerably older than me – and rather more smartly dressed, with bow ties and shimmering jewellery – but I relaxed when I reminded myself we were all there for the same reason: love of the piano.

'Oh,' I said, spotting a familiar face crossing the foyer. Mr Akino. I couldn't be sure whether he'd failed to see me or was simply avoiding me, but before I could call out to him, he'd left the foyer and walked in his purposeful way into the hall.

As I strolled through, checking my ticket against the numbers on the backs of the seats, I heard someone call out my name, 'Tomura-*kun*.'

I looked up.

'So you came!' It was the managing director of our company, in a smart and well-fitting dark suit, eyebrows raised dramatically, an exaggerated smile on his face. 'Where's your seat?' he asked.

'It should be around here somewhere.'

It was towards the rear of the hall, in the middle.

'I'm thinking this might be your first recital in this hall?'

'Yes,' I replied.

The MD leaned over and whispered in my ear. 'The acoustics are better by the wall.'

'I had no idea.' I raised my hands, fingers spread. I wished somebody had told me earlier.

Seeing my disappointment, the MD glanced at the crumpled ticket in my hand. 'If this is your first concert, you should hear it in a better seat. Shall we switch?'

I said no, there wasn't any need, but thanked him anyway.

To my amusement, he looked relieved.

When I'd finally sat down in the correct seat I spotted Mr Akino a few rows in front of me, over on the right-hand side. Which raised a question. Why would he sit so far over on the right as you face the stage? If you were keen to get a proper view of the pianist, wouldn't you choose a seat on the left side, where you could see the movement of the pianist's fingers and the expression on his face? I looked back towards the stage, and there was the beautiful gleaming black piano Mr Itadori had tuned yesterday, standing gloriously in the centre. From Mr Akino's seat, the piano completely obscured any view of the pianist.

The answer slowly dawned on me: he didn't care if he could see the pianist – possibly it was better that he couldn't. He wanted to concentrate solely on the sound. If you considered the direction of the lid of the piano, it was natural that the sound would resonate towards the right. I regretted picking a seat in the middle without giving this proper consideration.

My heart contracted a little as the lights in the hall dimmed and the pianist appeared on stage. He was a silver-haired man, more imposingly built than I had imagined from listening to him on CD. The applause subsided and he seated himself elegantly in front of the keyboard. He threw the tails of his jacket over the back of the piano stool, and adjusted his feet in front of the pedals, leaving his left foot on the floor, his right foot balanced lightly and in readiness on top of the pedal. A moment of stillness. He placed his fingers on the keys, lifted his wrists, and began to play.

In an instant any thoughts about where I was sitting were blown away. It was beautiful. Overwhelmingly beautiful. The physicality of the piano, its voice, the expression. From the black forest on stage something exquisite was flowing and filling the hall.

I tried listening to the tone with the thought that Mr Itadori had created it but even that proved futile. If tone has colour, this one was nearly translucent, or rather the sound took on whatever colours and form the pianist desired, from one moment to the next. Together we were lifted up, as though we had become one with the music, as though we too were part of it.

If I hadn't known, I probably wouldn't have thought this was a sound that Mr Itadori had called into being. But I understood. The ideal sound is in harmony with the person who plays the instrument – a sound that allows the pianist's own talents and personality to shine most brightly. No one thinks about the skill of the tuner. And that is perfectly fine.

As the last of the applause from the audience slowly faded away, I was left perfectly happy, even a little intoxicated. I rose from my seat and joined the flow of people exiting the hall. The MD was among them.

'So how was your first concert?' he asked.

'It was wonderful,' I said, unable to find a more colourful word to describe it. 'The piano was amazing.'

The boss was all smiles. 'Loving the piano, loving music – that's what it's all about.'

I couldn't imagine that anyone listening to this evening's music hadn't loved it.

'Though I do get the feeling that Mr Itadori is loved a little too much by the pianist.'

I followed the MD up the curved staircase to the foyer.

'The maestro depends on Mr Itadori so much, he calls him simply *Itadori* – I imagine *he* can't relax at all during the performance.'

'Is Mr Itadori that close to the pianist?'

'Didn't you know?' Another dramatic raising of the eyebrows. 'Whenever he comes to Japan he calls for *Itadori* as his tuner. He developed a fondness for him back when Mr Itadori was training in Europe. He also accompanied him on concert tours of Europe, but unfortunately Mr Itadori hates flying. Once he had returned to Japan, he would only travel by land. He waits in this unremarkable, out-of-the-way town for the pianists to come to him.'

'Isn't that a bit of a waste?' I couldn't help but say. 'Wouldn't he be able to put his skills to better use in a larger city, where he could tune pianos so that more people could hear them?'

'You really think so?' As we walked through the foyer the MD chuckled. 'I'm surprised you think that way, Tomura-*kun*. Would a big city really be good for Mr Itadori? It's a stroke of luck for us and our community that Mr Itadori chooses to stay. And for you, too, of course.' He glanced at me, his eyes narrowing and serious now. 'There's such wonderful music in the world. And even people in this far-off town can enjoy it. I think it's better that people from the big cities fly here to enjoy listening to Mr Itadori's piano.'

He was quite right, and it challenged the way I'd been thinking for so long. City or town. Urban or rural. Large or small. Before the penny dropped, I'd been captive to a standard that had nothing to do with value.

I'm going to do my work right here, I decided, and I was determined to be proud of that.

'It's just that the concert was so wonderful I thought it'd be great if more people could hear it,' I said in a small and slightly defensive voice, trying to justify myself.

'I know.' The boss nodded, smiling once more.

It Needs to Sound Lively

BACK IN TUNING SCHOOL, whenever I thought I'd got all the notes in tune, my instructor would sound each and every note. He'd mark an X in chalk on each key that wasn't in tune. And it would be a row of X, X, X, X, X, X – a whole never-ending line of them. Not a single one was in tune. During the two years of training, through constant practice, gradually the number of Xs decreased, and somehow I was able to get rid of the lot by the end of the course. Finally, I was on the starting line.

I always remember this. Adjusting the fluctuation of sound waves and the pitch – that's something anyone can master with practice. I was told in no uncertain terms that it had nothing to do with innate skill but was entirely through effort. It didn't matter whether you could play the piano or not, whether you were zealous, or whether you had a good ear. As long as you practised, anyone could do it.

The whistle had blown and I had begun the long race, but I wondered: how far had I moved from the starting line?

'The sound is much clearer and distinct now, I think. Thank you.'

Thanks and a bow of the head.

Once I'd left a client's house, I always made a point of jotting down notes about the job, often as soon as I got back to the car. What condition the piano had been in, what sort of tuning I'd carried out, what quality of tone the client was looking for.

Following this particular appointment I also noted the client's impression that the piano now sounded clearer and more distinct. The word 'distinct' was very important. Even if clients couldn't quite express what sort of sound they were after, I could read their desires from random comments they made along the way. Today's client had most certainly been looking for a clarity of sound even if he hadn't been conscious of this himself – he was so very pleased at the end of the job. I was recording a trail of evidence – a sequence of clues that had led me to this point.

Some people preferred a softer tone, some a sharper or more acute sound. If they were able to express themselves clearly, then I could tune the piano to fit what they wanted as closely as possible. The problem was that clients more often didn't know themselves what sound they wanted. Then, through a few stray hints, we both fumbled towards the sound we were after.

'It needs to sound lively.'

Although I was happy when this particular client, who'd been unsure of what he wanted, was pleased with the tuning I'd done, his final verdict left me confused:

'Thanks to you, it has a more mellow tone now.'

A lively sound and a mellow sound – how were these compatible?

The client, not noticing my puzzlement, continued, 'It's as though a flat tone has become more rounded.'

Ah, now I finally understood. Apparently he meant that a slack, relaxed kind of sound had tautened up, become rounded like a crystal-clear drop of water. When I finally understood this, a ray of sunshine seemed to break through. How ideal it would be if we could communicate solely through the voice of the piano.

People often asked me to make the sound brighter. At first I didn't give it much consideration. I merely thought that there couldn't be many people who would be after a darker sound. But now I think differently. I've learned that the single word 'brighter' has many shades of meaning.

The basic A above middle C is set at 440 hertz for a school piano. Apparently the first cry of any infant in the world is projected at 440 hertz. Hertz means the number of times per second that the air vibrates. The higher the number, the higher the sound. Until the end of World War Two, A above middle C in Japan was set at 430 hertz. If you go back further in time to the Europe of Mozart's day, it was 422 hertz. It's gradually getting higher over the years. Nowadays it's often set at 442 hertz. Concert pitch for A above middle C for an oboe in an orchestra is set at 444 hertz, and since pianos tend to be adjusted to suit that, their pitch will probably climb even higher – nearly one whole semitone higher than when Mozart was composing. In other words, the sound we perceive now is simply no longer the same A above middle C.

There's no reason for standard pitch to change, but the fact that it's become slightly higher over time must, I imagine, indicate that people want a brighter sound.

'The way the standard pitch keeps on going up, it feels as though everyone's flustered and in a rush,' I said.

Mr Yanagi and I were at a takeaway joint near the office. He was counting out the coins on his palm as we waited for our salmon nori bentos.

'You're right. At the very least they want the sound to be brighter,' he said. 'I've seen that too in the last few years – how home pianos are shifting from 440 to 442 hertz. It'd be a little creepy, though, if the client had such perfect pitch they could tell a difference of two hertz.'

'Will the pitch get higher and higher, do you think?'

'That would be my guess.' Mr Yanagi said this playfully, but then suddenly leaned into me. 'You know, Mr Akino once said this to me: if you do your best to tune a piano for a brighter sound but the client wants it *brighter, brighter* still, then it's better to show them how to modify their own piano technique.'

'What do you mean?'

'Meaning, it's not good to rely entirely on tuning to get a brighter sound. Oh, thank you.'

The two bento meals were ready and Mr Yanagi smiled and patted his stomach hungrily. We grabbed the food from the counter and left.

Outside, the spring sunshine was spreading its rays through the trees. A gentle breeze carried with it the faint scent of vegetation.

'Simply striking the keyboard with a more confident touch gives greater clarity to the sound. I think he also recommended lowering one's centre of gravity to put more body weight behind the fingers so as to make the effect more resonant and distinct. In other words, not via tuning but through performance technique.'

I could understand that. Even if a client asked that we make the action of the keys easier because they wanted a brighter sound, there were times when this just wasn't possible. It's not that there would be an issue with the keyboard itself but that the pianist's touch was too light, so the piano would never ring out, no matter what we did.

'A simple adjustment to the height of the seat makes for a different sound, doesn't it?' I said.

'Yep,' Mr Yanagi responded with a quick nod.

Strictly speaking, this might lie outside the purview of our job of tuning. But by tweaking the height of the piano stool, the touch on the keyboard will seem easier and the sound brighter. The optimum height for the seat is based on the height of the pianist as well as on how they use their body when they play and the angle of their wrists and elbows in relation to the keyboard.

'I saw a film of a recital with two pianists performing a duet, supported by an orchestra. Something felt odd about it until I noticed that the two stools were set at different levels even though the pianists were of similar height.'

Mr Yanagi nodded again silently.

I continued, 'If you looked carefully you could see that the angle at which the pianists held their arms and the way in which they extended their elbows were different. I imagine they each hit the keys with different levels of pressure, too. I don't play the piano myself and hadn't noticed that before. I can only give limited advice, but when I'm tuning I always ask clients to sit down and play so I can adjust the height of their seat. That one small correction seems to brighten the sound.'

'Very true. The seat is often much higher or lower than it needs to be.'

Sometimes it's better for them to sit closer to the piano, or further away.

'However—' There's always a *however*. Sometimes no matter what you do or how hard you try, you cannot please the client. Often they don't react at all. 'Most of the time you don't know what they want.'

'Yeah, that happens.' Mr Yanagi gave a small smile. 'The thing is, we might be after 440 hertz, but that isn't necessarily what the client is looking for. They just want a beautiful A above high C.' He was right.

We walked on, carrying our bento meals in their plastic bags.

'I think it's a wonderful thing that all this can be expressed as 440 hertz. Each piano's different, but they're all connected by sound, all conversing through the same frequency.' I felt a little embarrassed by the end of our conversation, surprised by how much I'd spoken during our exchange.

We sat down on the concrete block beside the shrubbery in the car park. The endless winter had finally lifted and on sunny days we sometimes ate lunch here. It was still chilly, but after hours in a stuffy room, doing all the detailed work involved in tuning, it was refreshing to eat our meal in the fresh air and to chat.

Sometimes I'd recall how Mr Akino said, with feigned indifference, that all we needed to do was focus on the high and low notes. 'We might very well feel it's all a bit futile if, time after time, we put our hearts into improving the tone but the client isn't satisfied or simply doesn't notice. On the other hand, if you do a half-decent job and don't worry too much about the finer stuff, the client is usually perfectly satisfied. In short, the client doesn't care if you're giving it your all or not. Coming up with a good sound – that's our one and only mission. And if a client feels that a pronounced bass and treble sounds good, then there's nothing wrong with giving it to them.'

'But still—' The concern I'd had many times came back to me.

'What's wrong?' Mr Yanagi pulled his disposable chop-sticks apart and looked at me, amusement on his face. Apparently I'd spoken my thoughts aloud.

'No, it's nothing.'

But it wasn't nothing. What I was thinking was: doesn't this crush the possibility? The possibility of encountering a truly sublime sound? A sound that sends a shiver through your heart, as had happened to me back in the gym of that sixth-form college?

Sure, I might not be able to produce that sound myself – I was still a beginner – but if you don't make that your goal, you will never get there.

Achieve a Sense of Harmony

THE TEMPERATURE HAD SHOT UP, and just stepping out into the fresh air was enough to make me feel as though I hadn't a care in the world. I didn't normally go out on my days off but was glad I'd done so today – glad I'd made some plans.

I imagined how the leaves of the white birches at home must all be emerging now, and as I walked, I pictured my small village up in the mountains. I recalled the spring when I left and my younger brother stayed behind. The village had only a single small school for compulsory education. There was no sixth-form college, and so at fifteen I had to leave the village, the mountains and my home. In that sense it should have all been expected. About a year ago, my brother left home too.

When I came home to visit, I felt I didn't fit in, especially when my brother was talking happily with my mother and grandma. I'd often escape out of the back door, wander aimlessly through the forest just beyond our house, breathing in the thick green fragrance and listening to the leaves rubbing against each other. Only then would I finally relax. As I trampled the dirt and grass, and listened to the birds calling in the treetops and the distant cries of animals far off on the mountainside, my perpetual queasy sensation of being out of place and not knowing where else to go would gradually melt away. Only on these solitary walks would I finally feel welcome and at peace.

To my joy and surprise I discovered something similar with the piano. A feeling of acceptance, a sense of harmony with the world. Words were not enough to express my wonder at this, so I sought to express it through sound. Perhaps I was also trying to replicate the atmosphere of the forest through the medium of the piano.

A small sign on the pavement led me down some narrow stairs to what looked like a basement venue. At the entrance, I handed over my ticket.

'Go in and find somewhere to wait for me,' Mr Yanagi had said when he'd handed me the ticket the day before, but it was hard to know where an appropriate *somewhere* was. The ticket said a drink was included with the price of admission, so I decided to get one. The rest of the crowd seemed a little older than me and cooler, too. By *cooler* I mean that some had dyed hair – blond or red – or spiky hairdos. These people were hip and had confidence, totally unlike me. I felt a little awkward mixing with them and stood to one side.

Sipping my ginger ale from a paper cup, I studied a poster with the names of the bands that would apparently be playing. Seven bands – none of which I'd ever heard of. I wondered which one Mr Yanagi had come to hear.

The ginger ale was overly sweet and I left half of it. I didn't know where to throw the liquid away and put the cup back on the counter. The woman behind the bar glared at me. I had no idea what to do in this situation.

I pushed open the heavy door of the venue. People had gathered near the stage, which was dimly lit, with a couple of mike stands, huge amps and speakers, and a drum kit at the back. There were two electric keyboards as well, but no piano.

'The show will begin soon,' a man announced and the crowd in the bar area flooded excitedly on to the floor near the stage. Shoved from behind, I was carried along with the current. There was still no sign of Mr Yanagi.

The low background music from the PA system suddenly stopped and there were cheers. Shrill voices and deep voices. At this rate I'd never be able to find Mr Yanagi. People pushed from all directions. The stage lights came on, getting an even louder cheer. The band members came on from backstage. One guy had a guitar under his arm, another held his drumsticks over his head. Another . . . my eyes skipped back to where I'd just been looking. I'd seen that bloke with the drumsticks somewhere before. Why did he seem so familiar?

My little yelp of surprise was drowned out by the sound of the guitar, and above all by the regular thump of the drums as Mr Yanagi began to beat the hell out of them.

The steady rhythm surged right up my spine, goaded on by the throbbing bass, the guitar work growing faster and faster and the vocals shrieking alongside. Enough to numb all your senses. The crowd was leaping, bouncing around, cheering, singing along, yelling, everyone doing their own thing. Every twitch of the vocalist's body worked the audience into a greater frenzy. Probably able to feel the crowd's reaction, Mr Yanagi, sweat flying, seemed to be having the time of his life.

The thing is, though, the sound was too loud, so it was impossible to judge if it was any good or not. Maybe it didn't matter. Up on stage Mr Yanagi looked positively radiant.

The band played four numbers and finished their set to a wave of cheers and applause. The house lights came on and the tension in the room eased. I used the opportunity to wend my way through the crowd into a clear area.

Mr Yanagi in a band? And playing the drums? That was a shocker. I mean – *drums*? My first thought was that it had to be bad on the ears. Even after they stopped playing my ears were still ringing.

Tomura-kun?

It sounded as if someone was calling my name. Probably just imagining things. It seemed as if lots of people were speaking to me, some close, some far away, but it was an illusion. I'd have to be careful about the noise level at live performances.

Tomura-kun?

I was hearing things again. It had all been too much for my ears. Would Mr Yanagi meet me here? Or would he be out at an after-party with the other band members?

'You're Tomura-*kun*, aren't you?'

Someone actually *was* calling my name, right next to me. I turned around and saw a woman I'd never seen before. Short hair, long neck, a really gorgeous woman.

'I knew it.' The woman grinned. 'My name's Hamano. I've known Yanagi – Yanagi-*kun* – for a long time. He told me to wait here for you. You're exactly how he described. I recognized you straight away.'

For a moment I wondered how he might have described me. But I was helpless in the glow of that broad smile. 'Uh, nice to . . . meet you,' I stammered.

'Likewise.'

We bowed to each other. She'd called him simply 'Yanagi', in tones of such pride and conviction that his name sounded quite different on her lips. I had a feeling that my Mr Yanagi was poles apart from her Yanagi.

The door to the hall shut again. The next band must be starting their set.

'Mr Yanagi's drumming was really good, wasn't it?' I ventured.

'It's so precise, isn't it,' she said. 'Like a metronome.'

I nodded. 'Precise and powerful – he really throws himself into it.'

Miss Hamano gave a sweet smile and lit a cigarette. 'Yanagi is fond of metronomes.' She chuckled. 'He might get upset if he finds out I told you.' Elegantly, slowly, she exhaled her smoke. 'I've known Yanagi since we were kids. We've been going out for nearly fifteen years. We know everything there is to know about each other.'

How wonderful that would be, I thought, *to have a beautiful woman like this know everything about you, and to know everything about her in return*. But I couldn't think of anyone who was like that for me – beautiful or otherwise.

A silver ring glinted faintly on the third finger of her left hand, the one in which she held the cigarette. This must be the one Mr Yanagi had wrapped up with a ribbon and given to her.

'Tomura-*kun*, please take good care of Yanagi for me, OK?'

'To be honest, he's the one who looks after me!'

Miss Hamano's lovely lips straightened. 'You might not know it to look at him, but he's quite sensitive.'

'Really?'

'He used to hate public telephones.'

Had I heard her properly? The loud music had left my ears ringing. I looked at her so blankly that Miss Hamano laid her hand on my arm and explained further.

'They make public payphones those garish colours, don't they, so they stand out? He hated the greenish-yellow colour – said he found them quite hideous.'

I couldn't catch everything she said and wasn't completely sure what she was talking about. The word 'hideous' sort of hung there in the air. 'What do you mean, he found public payphones hideous?'

Miss Hamano stubbed out her cigarette. Her nails were dark and glossy.

'He would feel sick whenever he spotted a payphone when he was out in town. Overly sensitized, I suppose. He sees all kinds of things he shouldn't – I don't mean like ghosts or anything, but things that flood his senses. Like flashy billboards, for instance, which he also couldn't stand. He found them completely overwhelming.' She looked at me as if to check that I was following.

'When he couldn't handle phones and billboards and that sort of thing, what did he do?'

'He'd go straight home to bed.'

This felt a little over the top. Then again, I guess it was a fairly mild reaction to things you really couldn't cope with.

'You'd think someone like that wouldn't survive. I was afraid he'd end up a total hermit.'

I'm really glad he avoided such a fate. He must have fought so hard to endure in a world full of things he couldn't deal with. What had rescued him? I wondered. Was it her?

'One other thing – sometimes when he used to walk about outside, the ground would suddenly look absolutely filthy to him.'

'You mean roads that hadn't been cleaned?' I really didn't get it.

'Whatever road he was walking down – in other words: the world. Life. He said it all just looked so utterly filthy to him.'

She sounded as if she was joking. I was having trouble seeing any similarities between her Yanagi and the Mr Yanagi I knew.

'Rude, don't you think? It's like he was saying that I, walking along without a care, didn't mind being filthy.'

'The Mr Yanagi I know is very kind and reliable. I don't get the feeling that he's over-sensitized.' I was trying to be careful with what I said.

'True enough,' she said. 'But it wasn't easy to get him to that point. And he was also going through adolescence, which amplified everything. Back then everything made him feel sick. He was desperately looking for a place to escape to. But there was no safe place he felt at ease in, where his nerves wouldn't get frazzled. Going home and pulling the covers up over his head seemed the best strategy to him. When that wasn't an option he'd crouch down on the floor, shut his eyes and stop up his ears. He wanted me to rub his back for him, and I can't tell you how many times I did that.'

I couldn't picture the Mr Yanagi I knew in such a state.

'The metronome saved him,' Miss Hamano said, in a seemingly playful tone. 'You know the old-style metronomes, don't you? The analogue kind you wind up? He said he had discovered that listening to a metronome calmed him down. "Even if you're not with me, Hamano," he told me, "I'm OK as long as I have this." He'd spend the whole day winding it and letting it *tick tock, tick tock* away. When I was with him it just about drove *me* crazy, though.'

So a metronome was his saviour. It felt as though we'd finally arrived at the Mr Yanagi I knew.

Clinging to something, using it as a crutch to help keep you upright. Something that brings order to the world. That elusive thing with which you can survive, and without which you can't.

'I think I'm beginning to understand,' I ventured.

I recalled the gym back at my school and the moment when I first heard the sounds Mr Itadori made with the piano, and how I had then thought, *If only I can own this sound, then I can live.*

Miss Hamano used her straw to scoop some of the flakes of ice from her iced tea into her mouth and crunched them. 'The next thing was—' she started cheerfully, but as soon as she did, Mr Yanagi appeared.

'Hey, Tomura!' He sauntered briskly over to me, his face flushed. 'How was it? Did you enjoy it?'

'I thought you'd take a little longer to get out,' Miss Hamano said lightly. She stirred her drink with the straw.

'Well, I didn't want to keep you two waiting so I came out as fast as I could.'

'Your drumming was great, Mr Yanagi.'

He seemed pleased. 'Shall we go and grab a bite?' He invited me as though it was a matter of course, but I declined.

Miss Hamano looked surprised. 'Oh, but you must come! We'd only just started talking. We haven't reached the good part yet.'

She seemed a little anxious, and Mr Yanagi said, 'What were you two talking about?'

'We were talking about discoveries,' I replied.

Miss Hamano laughed.

I bowed to the two of them and climbed the stairs up from the basement to street level.

Miss Hamano was there before his discovery. She'd been in Mr Yanagi's world from the very beginning. Which is why, I thought, he was able to relax enough to find the next thing in his life.

I could imagine the discovery that followed the metronome. Something else that would help him calm down. That would help him endure even when Miss Hamano wasn't around to rub his back for him. A tuning fork or drums, or perhaps it was the piano. As long as he had that one thing, he could look for the path ahead, even in the dirtiest of worlds. It wasn't a tool to help him avoid any horrors; it was the power to deal with them. Through a series of discoveries *Yanagi* became the Mr Yanagi I knew. The emotions he felt when tuning a piano, creating sounds, sending these out into the world – that was what allowed him to forge ahead, head held high.

Had Mr Yanagi accepted this seemingly filthy world? Or had it accepted him?

Emerging from below ground, the town looked dazzling. The sky was bright and clear. A very pleasant April.

III

Not Quite
Intermediate

Stick with the Menu

IT ONLY SNOWS ON WARM days in Hokkaido. On extremely cold days the skies are a dazzling blue and clear as can be. It was May now and the unseasonal snow seemed to have lent the town a boisterous air.

'Snow! In the middle of May!' Mr Yanagi gazed ruefully up at the sky. 'Weather like this will really play havoc with the trees.' The buds on the cherry trees had only just started to swell, and now they were covered with a thin layer of snow. 'I do hope they'll still blossom.'

Of course, snow at this time of year was not at all unusual in the mountains. There would be snowfall after the Golden Week holidays in early May, and once that melted it marked the arrival – at long last – of spring. In March we'd be on the lookout for more snow, then we'd limp through April and at last we'd reach May. The last of the grimy slush would melt away and the cherries would finally blossom as everything started to warm up.

'How it affects the spectacle of our beloved cherry blossom is one thing,' he said, 'but the snow also plays havoc with all the pianos we've gone to such infinite trouble to tune.'

In homes where the piano is in frequent use, it's good to get it tuned every six months, but most homes can get by with a once-a-year tuning – ideally at around the same time, to ensure the temperature, humidity, atmospheric pressure and so on remain constant.

Today Mr Yanagi and I were on our way to tune a piano. More precisely, the piano required a level of retuning. That was depressing enough, but to top it all, we now had to contend with the snow.

'As ever, Mr Yanagi, your tuning is the best.'

The client tried out the piano and seemed pleased with its smoother tone. His name was Mr Kamijo and he was the pianist in a bar. 'You tuned it exactly as I requested. No, actually, you've made it even better. I'd love it if you could come over every day.' He stroked his goatee rather theatrically.

Mr Yanagi gave a modest bow and thanked him.

'You know, I've been having off-days recently,' Mr Kamijo continued. 'Times like that, I can never decide whether it'd be better to go for a lighter, more mellow tone to cheer me up, or a darker one to match the gloom of my mood.'

It was some weeks ago that I'd taken on this client – or rather since Mr Yanagi had handed him over to me. I didn't know the details except that he was a professional pianist. And yet his piano didn't seem to be played much and wasn't looked after. He didn't hang around while I tuned it and requested no particular sound before leaving me to it.

The previous week he had called the shop to complain that the piano's lack of resonance must be the result of the different tuner's work. As it had been over a month since the original tuning, however, the guarantee period for a free retune had officially passed.

'Fine,' he'd said, 'but I just want the original tuner to do the job.'

So there I was, watching as Mr Yanagi worked on the piano. He'd told me I didn't need to come, but I wanted to see what he did with my own eyes. He was, as ever, wonderfully skilful. As I watched him briskly tuning, I understood why people felt in safe hands when they left things with him. And conversely, I could well understand why they were uneasy leaving their piano in my hands. Even if I produced identical results, I just lacked the same easy confidence.

'You know what *improvisation* is?' Mr Kamijo said, using the English word. He was addressing Mr Yanagi.

'Ad libbing.'

'I knew you would know, Mr Yanagi.' Mr Kamijo gave a fake smile. 'At the bar I often get requests to improvise. The pieces they want me to ad lib are all pretty tough but I find this type of challenge a real thrill.'

'I see,' Mr Yanagi murmured, without looking up from his work.

'You know what I'm trying to say, don't you? What's important is the improvisation. The audience want you to read their intentions and play in tune with their own wishes and desires at the time.'

'We also do our best to respond to a client's requirements.'

Mr Kamijo must have been put out by Mr Yanagi's rather blunt response as the smile had vanished from his face.

'I mean, this young man is an apprentice, isn't he?' he said. 'Why send *him*? I make my living with the piano, you know, and I've always brought my custom to your company. Do you take me for a fool?'

Mr Kamijo had raised his voice, and I was now staring at a small hole in the floorboards.

'Tomura is not an apprentice,' Mr Yanagi responded firmly. 'He is an official tuner in our company.'

'But he isn't any good,' Mr Kamijo insisted.

'He's young, admittedly, but he knows what he's doing.'

Mr Yanagi didn't budge an inch, but still Mr Kamijo stood there, arms folded, shaking his head.

The retune came over a month after I'd originally tuned it. Mr Yanagi insisted that Mr Kamijo pay the set tuning fee on this occasion, too, even though he might never ask our company to tune his piano ever again.

∽

MR YANAGI AND I WALKED back through the swirling snow to the car park.

'I'm sure that a pianist would get the best sound if he had his own exclusive tuner to adjust his piano every day according to how he feels,' I said.

I had the vague sense I was signposting something on the road ahead with this statement.

'For concert halls, perhaps,' Mr Yanagi said curtly. He was clearly in a bad mood. 'I don't think changing the tone according to your mood on a particular day is the way to go at all. The piano is simply not that sort of instrument.'

He might be right. There are limitations on how a pianist can determine the sound of his instrument. Each piano has its own individual personality. And so do pianists. The optimal sound comes through finding a balance between the two. All a tuner can ask is that a pianist trust in that collaboration between himself and his instrument.

'Say, for example, there's a really fabulous restaurant.'

Here we go again, I thought, bracing myself. Mr Yanagi and his metaphors. Most of which had to do with food.

'It'd be so wonderful if they prepared the dishes on the menu according to your physical condition and how you felt that particular day. But if you trust that the restaurant is good, you're not going to ask them to adjust the flavour to suit how you're feeling from one day to the next. Would you agree, Tomura?'

'You're right, I wouldn't.'

'My point exactly. You go along with what's on offer on that menu. The customer has to be confident that he's about to enjoy a reliably delicious combination of dishes.'

I nodded silently – I knew exactly what he was getting at. But he was able to say this because he had such innate confidence in his own ability.

'With restaurants, of course, they need you to enjoy the food from the very first bite.'

'Right.'

'A really skilled chef must take great pains so that not only is the first bite delicious but also the dish continues to taste wonderful, right until the moment you're scraping the plate. It's exactly the same with the sound of the piano. You want the first note to take the listener's breath away but you also want them to enjoy every last note, right to the very end.'

Not an easy assignment – a taste or a sound that you love from the very first moment, that you still find appealing as it fades into your memory.

'If the tuner lacks focus, though, there's no way they'll manage to create a sound that tugs at the listener's heart-strings from the very first note.'

Mr Yanagi looked over at me, biting his lip. 'Don't let it get to you.' He patted me on the shoulder. 'You didn't do a bad job at all.'

'Thank you.'

I felt guilty about worrying him. But if my job had been up to scratch, then why did the client complain?

'He was just in a bad mood. It often happens. There's nothing to be gained by fretting about it.'

Mr Yanagi seemed on the point of saying something else. He gazed up around the edge of his umbrella at the white sky as he walked, and avoided my eye. 'Your hard work isn't all wasted, Tomura.'

'What do you mean? Of course not!' I blurted out, more loudly than I had intended. Mr Yanagi seemed taken aback, letting out a little 'What?' of his own. We came to a halt and faced each other.

'I never thought that for a moment.'

I was being honest, and Mr Yanagi chuckled.

'I envy you, Tomura. So you've never thought it was a wasted effort?'

His chuckle turned into an enormous belly laugh, and by the time he'd put his hand on the door of the car he was properly roaring with laughter. He looked at me in wonder and asked, 'You've never regretted or looked back on something and wondered if it might have been a wasted effort? I mean, you don't actually feel the concept of something being wasted?'

'I do understand the word "wasted",' I replied hastily.

'Of course you do.'

'But I don't understand what it refers to.'

It felt to me as though nothing was a waste, but at the same time everything was on some level a colossal waste. Even working with a piano, and me just being here.

'Look,' Mr Yanagi said, opening and closing his black umbrella to shake off the flakes that had settled.

Hokkaido people don't usually bother using an umbrella when it's snowing, but we always tried to carry one to protect our precious cases of tuning tools. 'So you don't feel the concept of something being a waste. Take that a step further and it means you don't truly know the word "waste".'

He was climbing into the car, and for some reason a look of wonder came over his face. 'You don't know much, Tomura. And yet I feel, conversely, as though you've taught me something remarkable and new.'

'Well, you're welcome,' I said vaguely, and started the engine.

There's no shortcut through the forest. The only way forward is to keep honing your skills, little bit by little bit.

There were times, however, when I wished – with the utmost fervour – that I was blessed with a miraculous pair of ears and miraculous fingers. Couldn't those all of a sudden blossom for me one day? How wonderful it would be to actually manage to produce with these hands the kinds of sounds I imagined in my mind. The place I was heading for was so deep within the forest. If only I could get there in a single bound.

'But I still don't think anything's a waste.'

The car inched forwards, scrunching on the thin layer of unseasonal snow as it travelled.

'Sometimes I get the feeling, Tomura, that you're only pretending to be apathetic, and that really you're quite the greedy fellow.' Mr Yanagi tilted his seat back and stretched out leisurely, sighing loudly.

If piano tuning was a totally individual act, you could think of it in terms of hitting a target. It would be fine to take a taxi to your destination instead of walking – as long as tuning was your only goal.

But a tuner's work is not complete once he puts down his tools at the end of a job. It only comes alive when the client plays the piano, and that is why you have to walk and take the slow route. You have to listen to the wishes of whoever is performing, and you can't expect to get there in a single leap without making any tweaks. You get closer as you check things, one step at a time. You tread that path with utmost care, which is why you leave footprints. At some point you'll get confused and need those footprints to retrace your steps. You work out how far back you need to go, and where you made your mistake, until you're satisfied with the adjustments. And you can take someone's request into consideration and retune on their behalf, too. You will struggle mightily, remember with your ears and your body where and how you went wrong, but en route towards your chosen goal you can still listen to another person's desires and make those wishes come true.

'Oh.'

I said this more or less to myself, but Mr Yanagi, who'd been resting with his eyes shut in the passenger seat beside me, sat bolt upright.

'What's wrong?' he said.

'Nothing.'

'This car doesn't have snow tyres so drive carefully, will you? I mean, can you believe we're getting such a snowfall at this time of year?'

'A noodle place with a good reputation,' I replied.

'What?'

I thought, *They make the taste strong so the first bite is memorable because they don't know who'll be eating it.*

If they knew who was eating it, they could adjust it to suit individual preferences.

Aloud, I said, 'Shall we stop by at this noodle place, then?'

Mr Yanagi looked over at me and smiled. 'Why not? It's fine so long as we don't do it too often. So where is this popular noodle place, anyway?'

'I'm sorry. It's a metaphor.'

Disappointment washed over Mr Yanagi's face.

'I'll look for one – a place you'll really like,' I said.

Mr Yanagi's eyes stayed firmly shut after this.

As I drove I mulled over the day's activities. The client's remarks weren't just from spite, I decided. Something really *was* missing from the sound I had created. Mr Kamijo might not be the most diligent pianist, and might not have touched his piano at home for some time. But when he did, he sensed that something wasn't right – that the piano sounded different from usual.

Mr Yanagi was capable of things that were way beyond me. I knew this, but still it was scary to have a client confront and reject you like that. And it was doubly scary that I had no idea what it was I had done wrong or had missed.

'Scary? What is?'

I had thought Mr Yanagi was asleep and his sudden question gave me a jolt, not to mention leaving me embarrassed. I'd apparently spoken aloud the thoughts running around in my head.

'Weren't you scared when you first started out?' I asked. 'Didn't you wonder what you'd do if you turned out not to be any good at tuning?'

Mr Yanagi sank back in his seat, eyes narrowed at me. 'I suppose I wasn't. Or maybe I was.' His eyes opened wide. 'Are *you* scared?' he asked.

I nodded silently.

'That's all right. If you're scared, it'll spur you on. You'll work as hard as you can to polish your skills. Hold on to that fear a little longer. With so many things being thrown at you to absorb, it would be strange not to feel overwhelmed.' He chuckled. 'Don't worry about it, Tomura.'

'I can't help it. I'm always so anxious, so frightened—'

Mr Yanagi raised a hand to cut me off. 'Who is it who stays on to practise tuning pianos every day after work, hmm? How many do you think you've tuned altogether? How many books on tuning do you have piled up on your desk at the office? Read and study to that extent and you're going to know an awful lot. And you listen to piano music every single night at home, don't you? You'll be fine. But don't be put off if you feel anxious. Now's the time to be scared, if you're going to be.'

Even if I was afraid of the future, the present was even more frightening. I was still totally unable to tune a piano in the way I was desperate for.

'I wonder if you need talent to tune a piano?' I ventured, and Mr Yanagi turned in his seat to look at me.

'Of course talent's part of it.'

Just as I had thought, and it was a big relief to hear. I wasn't there yet, hadn't reached the stage where my talent was being tested.

I comforted myself with the notion that at least at this point talent wasn't what was needed – I must not let the word 'talent' distract me, or use it as an excuse to give up. Experience, practice, effort, knowledge, a quick mind, perseverance and passion. If I didn't have enough talent, I could make up for it with all of these. If one day in the future they were no longer enough for what I needed, then

I could give it all up – but the thought of this terrified me. It must be so frightening to admit finally that you don't have what it takes.

'You see, talent will out if you really love something. A tenacity, a fight in you that keeps you in the fray no matter what. Something like that. That's the way I've come to think of it.' Mr Yanagi spoke in hushed tones.

Don't Give Everyone a Harley

'Mr Akino,' I called out, but got no response. 'Mr Akino,' I called out again, and he finally noticed and looked up abruptly.

'What is it?' He lifted his hand to his ear and drew something out.

'What's that?'

'An earplug.'

The surrounding noise must bother him, I figured, but then it hit me. *It's for tuning. He's trying to protect his ears.*

'I do have a very sensitive pair of ears, you know,' Mr Akino said, poker-faced. 'So what do you want?'

'Would you let me come along with you?'

'On what?'

I wanted to learn what Mr Akino had dubbed the *boom-snap*, the high-and-low-end approach to tuning. I think I felt this way because I'd become so aware of the extent of my own shortcomings. 'I'd like to watch you while you tune, if you'd let me.'

I bowed and he pulled a long face.

'No, thanks, I'll find it hard to concentrate.'

'Please. I'd like so very much to come along and see you at work.'

I bowed again and he glanced down at the yellow ear-plug in his hand.

'I doubt you will find it very interesting.'

I took this to mean that, however reluctantly, he was giving me the go-ahead, and I thanked him heartily.

'Don't get your hopes up. It's just plain ordinary tuning.'

It's plain ordinary tuning that I wanted to know about – to see Mr Akino's plain ordinary way of doing things.

'I'm really looking forward to it.'

Still looking none too pleased, he'd already shoved the earplug back in place.

The house I visited with him the following day was, as advertised, an entirely normal one. A typical one-storey house with an upright piano, nothing special. But as I was to learn, the way Mr Akino tuned was far from ordinary.

First, he was amazingly fast, faster than anyone else I'd ever seen. A process that would normally take just under two hours he finished in half the time, and he made it look so easy. No wasted work, everything carried out with perfect precision. The tuning was over before I knew it, and there he was already replacing the front panel, and polishing up the keyboard and mahogany top board with a cloth. He returned a Beyer practice book to its place on the piano and called out to the owner, who was in a back room. The way he spoke to the lady of the house was so kind it was hard to believe he was the same stern Mr Akino I knew. They settled on an approximate date one year later for the next tuning.

He made his way out of the house, all smiles, but as soon as we were outside he reverted to the old grumpy Mr Akino I knew. We walked together to where we'd parked a little way off.

'That wasn't particularly interesting, was it?' he asked.

'Oh, it was,' I said. 'I found it really interesting.'

'Really? Not me.'

'I'm sorry.'

'No, you don't understand,' Mr Akino said, waving his hand to emphasize the point. 'I finished pretty swiftly, didn't I. I don't have to pull out all the stops in that household. Did you notice – a primary-school kid in the family using Beyer practice books?'

I'd noticed the practice book. That wasn't so unusual – primary-school pupils often used Beyer books in the early stages. Did he mean he was bored by the humdrum nature of the job?

'The height of the stool was a giveaway, wasn't it? The child in that family is in the upper years of primary school but still using a simple Beyer primer. Not exactly a kid who's crazy about the piano.'

'I guess so,' I said, although it didn't feel right to me. Just because the pianist wasn't that enthusiastic, it didn't mean it was OK to do a half-hearted job of tuning. And I liked Beyer as a composer, with his straightforward gentle melodies.

'I'll tell you one thing – I don't finish quickly because I am sloppy. I can handle a simple tuning in thirty minutes.'

I'd seen it with my own eyes so I knew it was true – Mr Akino's tuning was backed up by experience and technique, and he had a deft touch.

'I remember, Tomura, how you once said you couldn't quite swallow the idea of adjusting the tuning according to the client, right?'

He remembered. That was surprising. It's true I did think that, but I didn't recall ever saying it aloud. I never would have expected Mr Akino to give my reaction any thought.

'A person who usually rides a 50cc motorbike won't be able to manage a Harley,' he said. 'It's the same in this situation. If you adjust it so the touch is really sensitive, it'll actually make it harder for someone to handle who doesn't yet have the technique.'

As I unlocked the car I ventured to disagree. 'But if you practise, you can learn to ride a Harley.'

'It depends on whether or not you want to. At the moment this person can't and they're not showing any interest in trying. In a case like that, I think the kinder thing to do is to get the 50cc motorbike in the best shape possible for them.'

Who knows? He could be right.

'Personally, I like to adjust the action of the movement, so that when I play it has a more sensitive response. But with this sort of client I hold back and adjust the touch so it's duller and less resonant. If you have limited play in the action of the keys, any weakness on the part of the pianist will be less detectable. I intentionally adjust the piano so it doesn't resonate as much, bearing in mind the nature of the client.'

'I see.'

Mr Akino climbed into the passenger seat and quietly shut the door. 'It's really not very interesting. I'd much rather do a Harley.' He turned to stare out of the window.

I had nothing to say. It's not that he couldn't, it's that he didn't. Some people simply can't play a piano if it's too responsive. He wasn't making fun of the people who couldn't play it, but was actually being respectful towards them. No matter how well an amateur primary-school player can hit a ball, you can't just go handing him a full-sized bat. It's simply too heavy.

'It seems like such a shame, though.'

For Mr Akino, for the piano, for the primary-school pupil who only takes practice swings with a child's bat.

Mr Akino had his yellow earplugs in now and didn't reply.

Some of Us Are Blessed

'HE'S COMING NEXT YEAR!'
         Miss Kitagawa in our office was bubbling over with excitement as she gave the name of a famous pianist – a popular French performer whose nickname was Prince of Piano, or Master of Piano, or something like that.

'He'll be at the hall over there,' she continued.

By *over there* she meant over in another town, which had a wonderful concert hall. They had quite a few pianos, and whenever a famous pianist visited Japan, the kind whose recitals sold out months in advance, they would always use a Riesenhuber piano, the mark of a first-class concert hall. We had to accept that no great pianist would choose the modest hall in our own town – unless talked into it by Mr Itadori and his contacts – and that only tuners who worked exclusively for Riesenhuber were assigned to that particular breed of piano.

Mr Yanagi had overheard us and shrugged his shoulders. 'What can you do if it's in another town?' he said.

A towering presence in the world of piano manufacturing since the early days, the Riesenhuber company always dispatch their own tuners, regardless of distance. No local tuner is permitted to handle or even touch their instruments. Of course their employees are highly skilled, but they are also well known for their arrogance, unabashed in their contempt for anyone not connected with their illustrious firm.

'I've always hated the word "illustrious",' Mr Yanagi said, 'probably because it implies an elite I'll never in all my life have any connection with. I could stand on my head and still never be a match for them.'

'Standing on your head isn't going to get you to their level, Mr Yanagi. You have to stand on both legs, upright, or you won't be steady enough.'

Mr Yanagi stared at me dubiously as if he couldn't quite work out if I was joking or not.

'But we do have Mr Itadori on our side,' he continued proudly. 'They may be an illustrious firm and all that, but how many people do you think are better tuners than him? How many other people can make a pianist and their audience quite so happy? Even in the unrivalled Riesenhuber company, their tuners will be a mixed bag. I defy them to show me someone better than Mr Itadori. Don't you agree, Tomura?'

'Absolutely,' I replied. Mr Itadori's tuning *was* amazing. He was in a league of his own.

'The only ones who can touch this make of piano are employees of this company – have you ever heard of anything so ridiculous? The world is full of pianos and tuners. I could understand if they'd won some competition and the right to tune it. But they won't even let us compete. That's about all you can expect from a so-called illustrious company resting on its laurels. Not that I care one jot – that's not what we're aiming for.'

His eyes flickered as he mulled something over for a moment, but then he glanced up. 'Did I just say something cool?'

'Not really,' I said.

'Oh well, whatever.' He gave a small laugh.

I understood where Mr Yanagi was coming from, though. The feeling that they should appoint tuners who

were highly skilled, pure and simple, and not be compla-
cent. But still, wouldn't a technician from the company
that manufactured a particular piano, a tuner who worked
exclusively for that make, know their pianos best?

'Yanagi.' Mr Akino was looking at him from a desk
opposite and his eyes narrowed. 'So you are aiming for
– *what*, exactly?' He had now taken off his silver-framed
glasses and was cleaning them with a special cloth. 'I think
your logic is a little off.'

'Is that so?' Mr Yanagi's voice rose sharply at the end of
his question. He obviously didn't agree.

'We aren't the ones who set the goals,' Mr Akino said.
'Whether it's for a concert or a competition, the piano exists
on behalf of the person playing it. It's not the place of the
tuner to butt in.'

'I'm not trying to butt in. I'm just saying there should
be room for a goal we can all aim for.'

A goal we can all aim for. I, for one, couldn't see it.

'Also, the piano is not just for the person playing it,' Mr
Yanagi continued. 'It's for the people who will hear it, too –
for everyone who loves music.'

The office suddenly fell silent and you could certainly
have heard a pin drop.

Polishing the lenses of his glasses, Mr Akino looked
up. 'You think you said something cool, don't you, Yanagi.'

Sitting at the desk facing his, Miss Kitagawa covered
her mouth to hide a smirk.

'Ah, you got me there.' Mr Yanagi scratched his head,
trying to paper over the dispute by acting as though he was
simply clowning around. But the conversation wasn't over.

Uncharacteristically, Mr Akino had more to say. 'Every
tuner would like to have a world-class pianist play the piano

they themselves have tuned. But only a handful of us ever achieve it' – he paused for a moment – 'A handful of only the most blessed members of the trade.'

He'd said *blessed*, but wasn't he trying to say something else? About tuners who had reached a certain level of excellence and skill?

The phone on Mr Akino's desk rang, ending the conversation.

∽

IF IT WAS A QUESTION of being blessed or not, then I guessed I'd be in the unsuccessful category. The nuances of sound that a highly skilled tuner must be able to distinguish and what I myself had been brought up with were worlds apart. The soft *hotohoto*-plunk of ripe chestnuts falling to the forest floor. The rustling *sharashara* of leaves brushing against each other. The *chorochoro* trickle of snow sliding down the lengths of a thousand creaking branches. I'm not able to illustrate those sounds quite precisely enough in words: the ear recognizes sounds far beyond what can be expressed through simple onomatopoeia.

It's only natural that someone with an ear trained by playing the piano from childhood would develop a far greater acuity than someone who grew up ignorant of the highest-quality music.

But that wasn't what bothered me. I felt tripped up by Mr Akino's words, about to stumble and fall.

Did I really hope to have a world-class concert pianist play a piano that I myself had tuned? No matter how much I tried, I just couldn't picture it.

Even Pianos Deserve
Second Chances

THAT EVENING, MR YANAGI received a call. After hanging up he came over. 'They cancelled on me.' He was frowning, which was out of character for him. We often had cancellations, but I'd not seen him react this way before.

'Is something wrong?' I asked. And then it hit me. 'Was that the Sakuras?'

Yuni and Kazune's home.

'Yes, the twins' place,' he said.

'Maybe they had exams to study for.'

Or perhaps they had a performance coming up. There were times when they had to practise and couldn't spare the two hours it would take for a tuning. It was entirely possible they wanted to use the time to rehearse and so had put off the appointment.

'No, that doesn't seem to be the case,' he said. 'They didn't postpone it. They cancelled entirely.'

I felt my heart flutter a little. 'Maybe they were in an accident.'

The words came out without me thinking, and Mr Yanagi reacted harshly.

'Don't even joke about it.'

I couldn't help it.

'Do you want to call them?' he asked me.

I shook my head. I was too scared. Frightened I might hear something devastating.

Mr Yanagi walked away from his desk. He looked as if he might ring their home directly from his mobile. I didn't want to know. I'd realized there was another possible reason. Yuni and Kazune were perfectly fine and still playing every day. Perhaps they simply didn't want us to tune their piano any more. They'd decided to ask another firm of tuners to do it.

Sadly, that wasn't beyond the realms of possibility. But as long as Yuni and Kazune were both fine, well, that was far better than the alternative.

Mr Yanagi came back a little later. 'She can't play any more.'

I couldn't believe it. 'Can't play? *Who* can't?'

'I don't know. She didn't say. It seemed too awkward to ask.'

Yuni or Kazune – one of them – could no longer play the piano? Why?

'Their mother said, "My daughter's at a place where she can't play for a while, so we're going to leave the tuning for now."'

I didn't want to believe it. My memories resounded to the strains of their piano. I didn't even want to think about which one might have stopped playing, but I knew which one I most wanted to go on.

A huge and jagged stone seemed to drop into the pit of my stomach.

Kazune. I loved her playing. I wanted Kazune to go on playing the piano. But for that to happen, it had to be Yuni who had stopped. I was filled with guilt for even wishing it.

The office suddenly felt cold. I shook my head vigorously to dispel all these notions.

It's the same when you're willing someone on to win a piano competition – it means you're hoping another person is the loser. It's hard to condemn a wish, though – it doesn't mean it's going to come true. And if it does, the wish-maker can't be held responsible. Fruit falls from a tree whether I'm there to witness it or not. Somebody laughs, somebody cries.

I hoped Kazune would keep playing. As I wished this, I tried hard not to picture Yuni's cheerful, smiling face.

∽

THE NEXT DAY I PAID a visit to a new client. It was perfect timing since it kept me from brooding over the twins.

The piano was a very old upright. The client was still playing it but it was not known when it had last been tuned. All this I'd heard from Miss Kitagawa, who took the call.

'Tomura-*kun*, would you handle it?' she asked, and of course I nodded. I wanted to build up my client list and welcomed the opportunity. The more experience the better.

'There may be a few issues with this client,' she added.

Better that the client had issues than the piano. When the client had issues, that didn't necessarily mean the instrument did. But when the instrument had problems, that meant the client did too.

When pianos have not been maintained, it's very difficult to revive the original tone. In the worst cases they're rendered quite useless as musical instruments. When I've told clients their piano needed repairs, they've sometimes turned me down flat, which has felt wretched.

'But I'm sure it'll be – OK. From his voice I'd guess the man's in his twenties.' Miss Kitagawa beamed. If she said he seemed decent, then he probably was. I decided not to speculate about his 'issues' and wait until I met him.

I put the address into the satnav and headed off. The square, brown bungalow, typical of the area, stood on the shady side of the street, on a corner.

There was no nameplate outside but when I rang the bell a man of about my age opened the door.

'Very nice to meet you. My name is Tomura.'

He gave no response to my greeting.

The whole place was very compact. A narrow door led off from the hall to a small bathroom, with another to the kitchen. He led me through that and on to the living room beyond. The piano was right up against the wall on the far side, blocking off much of the window.

The client pointed at the piano without looking up, his shoulders thrust forwards. I wondered if he was unable to speak, but then I remembered he was the one who'd made the phone call. His jogging bottoms and frayed hoodie with its sagging neck fitted him like a second skin, and I figured this had to be the outfit he wore all the time.

Last tuned who-knows-when, this upright piano had lost its black lustre, the top board and upper panel both dull and faded. Aside from sheet music, a crowd of other items fought for space on the top board – pencils, magazines, books, even a tennis ball – but it was reasonably clean of dust, suggesting the instrument was indeed in routine use.

'I'll go ahead and look at it,' I said to the man, who still didn't meet my eyes, and I laid my tuning case on the floor.

Opening the fallboard of the piano, I tested a key and couldn't believe my ears. The note was way out of tune.

The key next to it was off, too. And the next one along, and the one next to that, and indeed all the rest of them. A faltering, hesitant sound, muffled, making me nauseous as I listened – not a single note in its rightful place. This was going to be a tough job, I knew. I wondered if I was up to it.

'I'm going to start now. It'll take quite some time, so please just do whatever you like. I'll call you if something comes up.'

The man didn't react to any of this.

Normally at this point I'd ask what sort of sound the client was hoping for, but there was no time for that now. It looked as though I'd use up all my allotted time simply getting it back in tune.

I began by removing the clutter from the top board, opening it up, and removing the upper panel. It was terribly dusty inside. A yellowing sticker on the inside of the side-board revealed that the piano had last been tuned fifteen years earlier.

Even so, I knew this piano hadn't been abandoned. There was evidence it was being played, but it was hard to imagine, considering the state it was in.

I cleaned up all the dust that had accumulated inside. Apparently this guy played with the top board open sometimes, because a whole variety of detritus had fallen down among the dust: a paperclip, a cap for a pro-pelling pencil, a rubber band, a thousand-yen bill and a faded photograph. Dusting the photo with a tissue, I found the image of a young boy, smiling shyly at the camera from his place at the keyboard of the piano. I placed these objects beside the magazines from the top board and my box of tissues.

Moisture seemed to have accumulated behind the piano where it leaned against the wall, causing some of the strings to rust, besides which a number of the hammer shanks were warped. Checking each one I worried about managing to fix them all before I could begin the tuning proper. It was hard to believe that none of the strings had snapped yet – I didn't feel at all confident of being able to restore this dilapidated old instrument.

Reaching out for another tissue to clean the dirt off the strings, my eyes fell again on the photograph, and I blinked in surprise. It was the young man. It sort of looked like him, and it sort of didn't, but I realized that the sweet boy in the photo was the same man who lived here now. The boy in the picture had such a different air about him that I simply hadn't made the connection.

I picked up the photo and studied it. Yes, the resemblance was there. *What could possibly have happened between then and now*, I wondered, *to change the smiling boy in the photo into this decidedly unsmiling man who can't look me in the eye or offer a single word?* Still, I had work to get on with, and no matter what shape a piano might be in, there was always hope.

There is always, *always* potential – even in a long-abandoned piano, cast aside in the worst conditions. If a tuner is called out on a job, that always means someone is planning to play their piano. No matter the circumstances, it will be ready for action once it's been through our hands.

And so I began, intent on getting this piano back to the best condition possible.

∽

THE SMALLNESS OF THE HOUSE meant I could sense the young man's presence throughout. Even focused on my work, ears listening intently to count the vibrations, I was all too aware of the man in the room next door, listening along.

I wondered if he was planning to sell the piano after it was tuned.

Hours later, I was finally able to call out 'I've finished!', and the young man appeared at once, his eyes still unable to meet mine.

'Several of the hammers are warped and some of the tuning pins have become loose. It's possible to repair them, but at this point I've just done a temporary fix.'

The young man kept his eyes to the ground throughout my explanation.

'Would you like to try it out?'

There was a long pause and then he gave a faint nod.

I had doubts that a person who wouldn't even look you in the eye would play in front of someone else, so was surprised when he tapped a note on the keyboard – middle C – with his right index finger.

That middle C was unexpectedly powerful, but you can't tell how well an instrument's been tuned from a single note. The man remained motionless, standing hunched over the piano. I was about to suggest that he try playing a short piece when slowly he turned around. His face wore an expression of complete surprise. For the first time, our eyes met for an instant, then he looked away again. This time he played middle C with his thumb, and then all the way up the scale – do, re, mi, fa, so, la, ti, do. His left hand now fished around behind his back in search of the piano stool. He dragged it towards the piano, all the while facing the keyboard. Carefully, he at last sat down to play the whole scale from middle C with both hands.

Normally it's hard to relax when a client is testing out a piano I've just tuned. I tense up, knowing my work is being evaluated right before me. But this time I felt calmer than before I'd started the tuning.

From his seat, the young man looked over his shoulder at me.

'How is it?' I asked.

I needn't have bothered. He was smiling – the young man was smiling, just like the boy in the photograph. Before I had a chance to feel his delight properly in my heart, he'd turned back to the piano and started playing.

Decked out in his grey jogging bottoms and hoodie, his tousled locks sticking out in all directions, he leaned forward with his large body and began to play. His tempo was so slow I didn't recognize it at first, but I soon realized it was Chopin's 'Little Dog Waltz'.

No story came through from the music at first, but gradually a little dog came into focus. I'd started gathering up my tuning tools and turned in surprise to look at the man. This wasn't a little dog, it was a big dog. Chopin's dog was based on some toy breed like a Maltese, but the one summoned by the young man was something larger and a little ungainly, more like an Akita or golden retriever. The tempo was too slow and the notes uneven, but it was clear that the young man, just like a boy or a little dog, was enjoying playing. Occasionally he'd bring his face close to the keyboard and appeared to be humming.

So there are dogs like this, too, I thought. *And pianos like this.*

Watching from the far side of the small room, I listened to the young man's playing, with all its intensity of emotion, and when the piece ended I couldn't help from breaking out in a heartfelt round of applause.

Music Is No Competition

LIKE PEOPLE, EACH PIANO has an environment best suited to it. Pianos in a concert hall, resplendent and bold, dazzle us with their gorgeous, peerless sound. At least that's what I thought. But who's to say that they're the most beautiful? Who decides that something is the cream of the crop?

Since that day, I've often recalled that young man in jogging bottoms who avoided my gaze. No one listened to him play and he sought no audience. My presence on that occasion was of no significance to him, but I was witness to the blossoming of his shuttered heart as he played. He enjoyed those frolics with the dog so much – the joyful embodiment of playing the piano.

A concert hall wouldn't have worked. That particular piano was destined to wait in that little house for him alone to play. And that was fine. That quiet, solitary joy was not something you could appreciate in a large auditorium. This was a piano that allowed someone to smell the scent of a little dog and to stroke its soft fur – music at its most noble.

I could picture the person who had taught the young man to play, and how much he had relished the task. Music is there to help us enjoy life, not as a means to outdo everyone else. Even if you do compete and a winner is picked – the person who enjoys himself the most is always the real winner.

There's no comparison between listening to music in a large concert hall with other people and being so close you can feel the performer's breath. It's not a question of which is better or more valuable. The joy of music resides in both, although the experience might be different. The glistening of the world as the morning sun rises, the glowing as it sets – who can say which is better? The morning sun and evening sun are the very same sun, yet the form of their beauty differs. That's what I figure, in any case.

You can't compare them. And it's pointless to try. An object that holds no value to many people can to someone else be utterly precious. The desire to have a world-class pianist play your tuned piano in a concert hall may be a noble goal for some – but I felt that my vocation lay elsewhere.

I would not aim to become a concert piano tuner.

It might be foolish to decide something like that at this stage. It takes years of experience, training, dedication – and even then only a handful of lucky people will ever make it. But denying that possibility now might be seen as a form of running away.

Gradually, though, it was becoming clear to me. Music is no competition – and if that's the case, it holds even truer for tuners. A piano tuner's work lies far beyond the realm of competition. If anything, a tuner should aim for a certain state of being, rather than a place on the podium, a ranking in some race.

Bright, quiet, crystal-clear writing that evokes fond memories, that seems a touch sentimental yet is unsparing and deep, writing as lovely as a dream, yet as exact as reality.

I would summon up those lines from the writer Tamiki Hara, lines I'd read so often they were etched in my memory. Saying them aloud raised my spirits. No other words could better express what I aim for in my tuning.

∽

A CALL CAME INFORMING ME my beloved grandmother was on her deathbed. I rushed back home to the mountains but didn't make it in time. She had already breathed her last.

The funeral was a small one, attended only by my family, a few relatives and the villagers.

My grandmother had been born in a poverty-stricken village, married young, and had settled in the mountains. She'd made a living in the lumber business, but had always been poor. Others who'd settled in the mountains at the same time had, one by one, left and moved to towns, leaving only a scattering of families behind. The lumber business failed after her husband died young, in his thirties, and she went to work for a friend who'd gone into livestock farming, and there she raised her son and daughter. Her daughter left the mountains after middle school and the end of compulsory education and later got married in town. Her son, my father, left to attend sixth-form college, as I did, but then returned to work in the local government office. He got married and then my younger brother and I were born.

That's all I knew about my grandmother's background. She was a hard worker and a woman of few words.

∽

OUT AT THE BACK, BEHIND our house, facing the woods, was a dilapidated old wooden chair. It had been there as long as I could remember. Grandma would sit there sometimes, staring out at the mysterious expanse of forest beyond. I didn't think there was anything to see besides a lot of trees, and always wondered what she might be looking at.

Now, back in the family home and staring out at the same scene, I felt someone behind me and turned around. My brother was walking over, winding a scarf around his neck as he approached.

'Wow, it's freezing,' he said, and came to stand next to the ancient chair where I was sitting, legs crossed. He looked around. 'It's kind of scary, actually, how nothing ever changes up here.' He laughed.

'Definitely,' I said and laughed with him. There was one difference, however – the white birches planted at the front of the house were far taller and more imposing than when we'd both lived here.

The wind blew and my brother flinched.

'You know, I went to the beach this summer,' he said.

'Yeah?'

'With guys from my seminar group at college.'

'Did you swim?'

My brother snorted and shook his head. 'I can't swim. You know that.'

Neither of us could swim. There was no pool in our little school in the mountains. There was a public pool in the local town in the foothills and some of my friends went there to learn, but when my brother and I graduated from middle school we weren't even able to float on our backs in the water.

'Have you ever seen the ocean?' my brother asked.

'Sure.'

Our school trip in middle school took us to the southern part of Hokkaido, where I saw the Sea of Japan in autumn. The tuning school was near a harbour, too. Even so, the ocean was a rare and special sight for me.

The wind picked up again, my brother shrank into himself a little further, and the leaves rustled boisterously.

'When I was walking near the sea, it sounded like the mountains at night,' he said.

I could hear my heart thump loudly. The sound of the mountains at night. Had I known how they sounded? I tried to bring it to mind, but all I could picture was a night in the mountains that was still, so very still.

'You know, like on nights when there is a gusty wind, like today, there's a sound? Trees swaying in the wind make a moaning sound.'

'Right.'

The sound trees make when they bend in the wind. The leaves tremble, the branches shake, tens of thousands of trees echoing each other. I remembered how my little brother, scared, would crawl under Grandma's futon covers.

'I heard the same sound by the ocean,' he went on. 'I looked around for the mountains, which didn't make sense since I was next to the sea. "What's that sound?" I asked my friends.'

'Yeah?'

'And they said it was the *roar of the ocean*.'

The roar of the ocean. I'd heard the term before. Although I hadn't known it was like the sound of the mountains at night. 'It's strange that the mountains and the sea would make the same sound,' I said.

Gazing up at the treetops, my brother chuckled as he pondered my observation. 'Do you think that when people who grew up by the sea come to the mountains they're surprised to hear the roar of the ocean?'

I looked up at the sky, which was now a faint purple. A pale moon peeked out from the edge of the mountains. Pretending to look at the view, I flashed a glance at my brother's profile. Had he always looked this kind and thoughtful? It felt as though I hadn't looked at him properly in years. My little brother, always blabbing about something. He'd been a handful and, being two years older, I always had to keep an eye on him. Before I knew it we'd conformed to a stereotype: me as the quiet, reasonable elder brother, him as the more outgoing younger brother everyone fawned over. I had never intended to be dissatisfied with that.

But now, looking at my brother's face, I could feel something stir in my heart. For it to have such an impact meant there had to have been something lurking there, unresolved. At school, my brother was always a little better than me in class, and a little better at sports. Had I been jealous of that? And of how our mother and grandmother seemed to love him just that tiny touch more?

'You seemed to feel guilty for not coming back to live here.' My brother turned to look at me and our eyes couldn't help but meet. 'When you told us you were going to be a piano tuner you looked sort of apologetic about it.'

'Did I?'

'You did. Grandma told you, "There's no reason to feel sorry. Don't worry," she said, "about whether you should take over here or not." She might have said the same thing to me, too.'

Taking over – *what*? I was about to ask, but kept my mouth shut. We were both born and raised here. If there was anything to inherit, hadn't we already inherited it inside ourselves?

'You always talked so big,' my brother said. 'It kind of surprised everybody around you.'

I looked at him, startled. 'I did?'

When had I done that? Talked big? It was my brother who used to brag. Making my mother and grandmother happy by describing some brilliant future that awaited him.

'Don't you remember?' he asked. 'How worked up you were, saying how the sound of the piano connected up with the whole world? The *whole world*'s not something people usually say. I haven't even seen the world yet.'

'Neither have I.'

But this is the world, isn't it? I can't see everything, but it *is* the world.

'You're always dealing in big things – the world, music and so on,' my brother said, and he laughed in a cloud of white breath. 'But this, here – this isn't the world. It's just a mountain. Since I left this place, I've never come across anywhere else quite so remote or out of the way . . . Wow, it really is freezing!' he added, rubbing his hands. 'I'm going to catch a cold if I stay out here, so let's go in,' he urged, and I stood up.

'Grandma said she didn't understand the piano or music, but since you were small you had always loved the forest – and even when you lost your way among the trees, you'd find your way home. So you'll be fine, she said.' My brother walked off after that, without glancing back. He seemed to be a bit worked up.

We got to the door of the house and he suddenly turned to me and said fiercely, 'You're always like that – so easy-going on the surface but hard to read underneath.' His face had reddened. 'Grandma was always so proud of you.'

I was about to say it wasn't true, but the words stuck in my throat.

'I hate this. Why did she have to die? With her gone I have no idea what to do.'

His voice was breaking into sobs, and deep-seated emotions began to well up in me. 'I hate it too,' I said, though it didn't sound like my own voice.

I realized at last that it was good to cry at times like this. And before I knew it, tears were sliding down my cheeks. I stretched my arm around my younger brother's back; he was larger than me now. How long had it been since I'd hugged him closely like this? Something I'd pushed away from my life had jumped right back into me. It felt as if the outline of the world had suddenly been thrown into sharper relief.

∽

EARLY THE NEXT MORNING I took a walk in the forest. Trampling down the undergrowth, I stroked the rough reddish-brown trunks of the Yeddo spruce with my fingers. I heard a jay screeching from the top of a tree. An overwhelming nostalgia swept through me, along with confusion. Had I really forgotten this place? Was my heart really no longer here? The wind picked up and the scent of the forest grew sharper in my nostrils. Leaves rustled, branches rubbed together. When the still-green needles

of the Yeddo spruce fell they made a sound that was outside any musical scale. I rested my ear against a rugged
trunk and could faintly pick up the suck of water being
absorbed up through the roots. The jay screeched again.

The sound of the mountain at night and the voice of
my brother echoed in my ears.

One of Them Is Frozen

MISS KITAGAWA ASKED ME to come downstairs, where I found Yuni, the younger of the Sakura twins, waiting for me. My heart did a backflip.

'Hello,' she said, smiling confidently and dipping her head in greeting as she always did. It made me want to rush right over.

'Are you OK?' I asked, trying to sound as casual as I could.

'I'm fine.' Yuni's cheerful voice was all it took to lighten my spirits.

It had been some time since the twins had cancelled the tuning. We'd heard that one of them could no longer play the piano, but otherwise not a word. I couldn't very well probe for further details, but it continued to weigh heavily on my mind.

When I'd first heard the news, I couldn't help but hope it was Kazune who could still play. I wasn't comparing the personalities of the two girls, it was purely about the piano. I loved Kazune's playing. I couldn't stand the thought of never being able to hear her play again. But I felt guilty, too, and bad for Yuni, which is why I was so overjoyed that she had stopped by. Happy that she looked so well. My guilt abated just a fraction.

The instant I saw Yuni's shining face, I knew. It was Kazune who couldn't play any more. It was Yuni's piano playing that remained. But still, seeing Yuni there in front of me made me very happy. I was genuinely pleased she was doing so well. If Kazune was OK, that would be enough.

'I'm sorry we cancelled all of a sudden the other day,' Yuni said, bowing, a solemn look on her face.

'Please don't worry.' Mirroring Yuni, I bowed my own head in response.

Smiling gently, she explained, 'They say it's a weird illness.'

The word 'illness' came so unexpectedly that I flinched.

'There are no other symptoms. You're just unable to move your fingers when you try to play.'

I was lost for words. I'd never heard of this condition. *That must be hard*. Should I say that? Or *I hope she gets well soon*? A little too casual. No matter what I might say, it would seem wrong.

'Will it—' *Will it ever go away?* is what I was about to say, but swallowed back the words. It was an insensitive question. And what good would asking that do? If, for some reason, Kazune would never recover, then asking her sister Yuni to respond to that was cruel.

But Yuni seemed to guess my question. 'I don't know if you can recover from it or not,' she said. 'Most of the time people don't, but it seems the doctors can't determine that for sure.'

Her matter-of-fact explanation sent a chill up my spine. *Kazune may never play the piano again*. I was utterly horrified by the prospect.

'Please don't look like that. I'm not that upset about it. Actually, it did really get me down to begin with, but it's OK because there's been a bit of improvement.'

I couldn't find a single thing to say, and felt miserable. At times like this you find out how generous and supportive another person really is.

'I'm so very sorry,' I finally said. I was infuriated with myself for not being able to react appropriately or give any meaningful response. 'Thank you for coming all this way to tell me.'

'You're welcome.' Yuni smiled.

She looked as cheerful as always, but I had no clue as to what storm of emotions was swirling about inside her.

'The reason I came today is because I wanted to ask your advice. It's about Kazune.' She lowered her voice. 'Ever since the start of the illness she's been so depressed. She doesn't even want to go into the music room. I don't know what to do.'

That made perfect sense. It would be strange if she wasn't upset.

'She's not even sick, but she won't play. It's awful.'

Yuni said this in such a flippant way, wrinkling up her nose, that it confused me. It didn't add up. After a moment, it dawned on me.

It wasn't Kazune who was unwell. It was Yuni. I had jumped to conclusions.

'Kazune is so angry about me getting sick.' She inclined her head a little, and then rephrased her words. 'She's not angry at me, but at the illness. She's angry that it made me unable to play, and now she can't either.'

I took a moment to digest the new situation. Then:

'What about *you*, Yuni . . . Aren't *you* angry?'

She seemed to be considering this. 'I *am* angry.'

'Mmm,' I said, in what I hoped to be a reassuring way.

Of course she was. But she must be confused, too, not knowing where to direct her anger.

'Kazune has to play even more, to make up for me not being able to. And yet . . .' She was unable to complete the thought, stood there with her mouth open, taking rapid and shallow breaths as if struggling to draw air into her lungs. In the same instant her dark eyes started to well with tears.

I wanted to reach out to her but my arms felt glued to my sides. I wanted to touch her, reassure her it was going to be all right. *It'll be OK*, I wanted to tell her. But there was nothing OK about it.

Before the tears could spill down her cheeks, she wiped them away with the back of her hand. *Go ahead and cry*, I thought, but I confess to feeling a little relieved, too, that I didn't have to watch the flow of her tears.

Someone cleared his throat nearby, and I turned to see Mr Akino strolling past, tuning case in hand. *We must make an interesting little picture*, I thought. *A sixth-form girl in tears and a total dunce frozen awkwardly to the spot.*

Yuni stood still for a time, head down, but when she looked up the tears had stopped. Her eyes and nose were red. A single strand of her soft brown hair lay plastered from forehead to cheek.

'I'm sorry. Thank you so much for listening.' She bobbed her head, then turned away from me, peeling the hair from her face, and headed for the door.

I didn't know what to do. I was still on duty. But even if I had work scheduled, I knew I'd regret it if I didn't talk more with her – right here, right now.

I ran after Yuni and caught up with her along the pavement, lightly grabbing the sleeve of her school uniform. 'I'll walk you home.'

'It's OK, I'm fine.' Yuni's soft smile was back in place. But even with her normal expression restored, I just couldn't figure it out: I couldn't read how she was feeling on the inside. Although she'd gone out of her way to come and see me at work, and going home so quickly must mean she felt let down by my reaction.

'Do you fancy a cup of tea somewhere?' I racked my brain for a suitable place to take her.

But Yuni flashed her smile at me again. 'Really, it's OK, don't worry,' she said.

I had no idea if she was turning down my offer because she wanted to, or because she thought she should.

'Well, be careful on your way home then.' I couldn't think of anything else to say. I gave a feeble wave as she walked away. She rounded the corner without looking back.

Soft flakes of snow began to swirl around me. We were nearing the end of May and something, somewhere, wasn't right.

I turned around to walk back towards the shop, and was just reaching out for the door of the staff entrance when, out of nowhere, I recalled the sunny skies of midwinter. A translucent blue, with the sunbeams lighting up the branches of the frozen trees and making them sparkle with silver. Days so bright they hurt your eyes, and you just knew the temperature was about to take a plunge.

In the mountain village where I was raised it sometimes dipped as low as minus thirty degrees. When it got that cold, just once or twice a year, the night before would see a sky full of stars. And the next morning, not a cloud to be seen. Everything frozen, just sparkling snow and ice. Your breath froze, your eyelashes stiffened, and if you were careless enough to open your mouth too widely your windpipe would close up with a sharp, stabbing pain.

I remembered that sort of frozen morning. The sunny days were the most frightening.

Kazune in torment. Yuni bursting out laughing. Yuni suddenly crying. Which one's heart was truly frozen? That was a question I don't think anyone could answer.

IV

FAR FROM ADVANCED

Surrender Yourself
to the Wind

'So I'm on the roof of a high-rise, standing alone on the wrong side of the safety barrier. My shoes are sticking out from the ledge; it's only eight inches wide. Way down below I see cars and what look like people strolling. I try to steady my nerves, keep my footing. Raising my eyes, I look up at the sky. The wind is blowing and I don't know how long I can hold on. Won't someone please come and help me?

'The heartless wind picks up. The building lurches to the side, but surely it's my imagination – buildings can't lean over. It's the wind whipping my body this way and that. I'm exhausted and my knees are trembling. I can't hold out for much longer.

'But I stand firm, still holding on. I refuse to look down, and somehow I'm hanging on. Another gust of wind, my body sways, the building tilts a little further. Time to give up? I'm going to fall anyway – but not yet. I must try to hold on a little longer, just a little longer. There's still a chance I might be saved.

'But the wind blasts again and my body is thrown from the building.' Mr Akino wrapped his bento box neatly in a red gingham cloth, then stowed it away. He looked up at me. 'So what do you think?'

I had no way of responding.

He was telling me about a dream he often had. 'It's always the same. For whatever reason I'm standing way up in some high, dangerous place. If I fall, it's all over for me, but all kinds of other awful things come along to make it even worse. The wind gusts, or the building leans over, and in the dream I know I'm going to fall any minute now. I try my best to hold on, to grab on for dear life, but in the end I always fall.' He explained it all so matter-of-factly.

'If you fall in a dream, do you die?' I asked.

Mr Akino inclined his head. 'I don't know. That's not really important.'

Then what *is* important? And why did he start telling me about his dreams anyway?

'I have the same dream over and over. In the beginning I would do everything I could to hold on. But even then, I still fell.'

'That's a pretty scary dream.'

'It's awful. I'd wake up covered in sweat. But gradually, even when I was dreaming I began to understand that I can't be helped, that I'll always end up falling. Struggling won't help. And over time I learned to give up more quickly.'

To my surprise, I saw the faintest glimmer of a smile on Mr Akino's face.

'I knew I could try to hold on, but once the wind picked up it was all over. The last time I had that dream—' He stopped and looked down, as if pondering something. 'I remember it really well, even now. At the end I was standing on the ridge of a high mountain. I realized this was the same dream as always, and even before the wind and rain came along I hurled myself down all on my own.' Mr Akino swept his index finger through the air in an arc from his eyes down to his desk. 'When I woke up that time I wasn't sweating at all. I thought – so that's what giving up means.'

'You mean giving up in the dream?'

'It's fairly easy to figure out, I imagine. The day I leapt down of my own accord was the day I decided to become a piano tuner.' He stood up. 'OK, time to go to work.'

~

I WATCHED HIS THIN BACK recede as he exited the office, and then remembered something and dashed after him. Mr Akino was already walking down the stairs, and at the sound of my footsteps he halted and turned around. I hurried down.

'How long did it take until you jumped down?' I asked.

'Four years,' he said without hesitation.

'Four years,' I repeated to myself in a low voice. That was a bit of a shock. Would Yuni, too, spend her days scared she would fall for the next four years? But then end up jumping by herself?

I remembered how Mr Akino had passed us the day when Yuni came to the shop and wept. He must have heard what was going on. In his own way, he was telling me it would probably take her a long time to give up on the piano.

I wanted to ask Mr Akino if he'd been afraid when he finally jumped, but I wasn't brave enough. Compared to the terror and despair you went through before you fell, jumping had to be the better option. For all I knew, his face may have been wreathed in the kind of smile he'd shown me earlier when he finally pushed off from the ledge. At least I hoped so.

I knew that Mr Akino had been hoping to be a pianist himself. And I knew a profession like that depended on how long and hard you tried and how passionate you were about it. Age mattered, too, and of course there was the issue of one's personality. But still, I resolved to do whatever lay in my power to help release Yuni from the clutches of some horrible nightmare she'd have for the next four years.

I followed Mr Akino as he left, and out in the car park I gritted my teeth and asked, 'Why did you give up on being a pianist?'

'Because I had a good ear,' he said. 'I had a good ear, so I could sense a world of difference between the playing of a first-class pianist and my own efforts at the keyboard. I always felt there was an unbridgeable gap between the melody I heard in my head and what my fingers produced. And I could never bridge that gap.'

'But thanks to all that an excellent piano tuner was born.'

I thought he was going to scoff, but instead his face broke into a wide grin.

'You've grown to be quite the smooth-talking young man, Tomura.' He laughed.

Looking nothing like the Mr Akino I knew, he opened the door of his car and drove steadily off.

∽

UNUSUALLY THAT DAY, I HAD two appointments with clients. It was after seven when I finally got back to the office and found a note on my desk from Mr Yanagi: *Good news!* I looked at the two words of black scrawl on the memo pad and wondered what this could mean. Was it about the twins? I called his mobile from the office, and he answered straight away.

'Hey.'

'By good news, do you mean—?'

Before I could finish, he said, 'Yes. They called, asking for an appointment. They want to restart tuning sessions.'

'By restart, you mean—'

He interrupted again before I could finish the thought. 'The Sakuras. The twins' place. Their mother called.'

'I see.'

So it *was* them. This was fantastic – how I'd been longing for this day.

'So they've started playing again?'

A short silence on the other end of the line.

'Well, at least one of them has.'

It had to be Kazune. *If only the two of them could play again*, I began to think, then reined in my emotions. If only one of them could play, that was certainly better than neither. Far better.

'She asked, if it's not too much of a bother, if you wouldn't mind coming along as well.'

'What? It's OK for me to come along?'

'The twins requested it, she said.'

So we fixed an appointment and visited the Sakuras' home a week later, late in the afternoon.

Mrs Sakura welcomed us with a warm smile. 'We've been looking forward to this,' she said.

The twins came out and bowed together. 'It's been so long.'

I thanked the stars for their cheerful voices.

'Sorry for all the trouble.'

'We're so happy you could come.'

'We are, too.' Mr Yanagi smiled back. 'We're extremely happy you asked us to tune for you again.'

Standing just behind him, I bowed in turn. For the whole time we hadn't heard from them, I'd felt as if there were a heavy stone lodged inside my chest. Now it was crumbling into dust.

They led us to the music room, and Mr Yanagi asked, 'Do you have any special requests?'

'We'll leave it up to you,' the twins said in unison.

'Well then, if there's anything you'd like to tell us, please feel free at any time.'

Once the girls had left, Mr Yanagi took off his grey jacket and draped it over the stool in front of the piano. It was a single stool now, I noticed, in place of the two that had stood there previously.

He opened up the newly polished black piano and began to tap on the white keys.

I wondered why they'd requested both of us, why they wanted me there too. Yuni had come to the shop and told me about her illness, so perhaps she had thought it was only polite to request my presence too.

While Mr Yanagi was tuning, all kinds of thoughts ran back and forth through my mind. This room was a little overly soundproofed. There was, of course, soundproofing on the bottom of the piano legs, but they stood on a deep-pile carpet, while two layers of soundproof curtains hung at the window. Was it not a terrible waste for the sound of the piano to be muffled like this? It must surely halve the glorious charm of hearing Kazune play?

While Mr Yanagi was busy laying his cloths out beneath the strings, I tried clapping my hands. A dry *bam* came out, but soon stopped. Hardly any reverberation at all. I drew back the curtains, which ran from the top of the window all the way down to the floor, and clapped my hands again.

This time the reverb clearly lasted longer. Surely when she played during the day it would be OK to open the curtains?

'Close those.' Mr Yanagi was crouched down by the piano. 'They're always closed, so I want to tune the piano with them that way.'

'But it's such a shame. It's better to play with them open.'

'As they were, please.'

I reluctantly closed the curtains. It blocked the light as well as the sound. I drew back the curtains again and the gentle evening light shone in.

'Tomura!'

'OK, OK.' I grudgingly closed them once more. I just couldn't shake the notion that it was a mistake.

'What are you, a child?'

That was the first time in years anyone had called me a child. A single laugh escaped me and I felt lighter somehow.

'What are you laughing at?'

'Nothing. I'm sorry.'

But there was mirth in my voice even as I apologized.

Not knowing why the twins had asked me to come, I watched as Mr Yanagi smoothly went about his tuning. His work was so very precise. Now that I was tuning myself I could really appreciate his labours, see what painstaking care he employed with each step of the process and marvel at his nimble fingers. There was no point in trying to imitate his technique – no one else could tune quite like him – but I was grateful for the opportunity to study his work at close hand.

Mr Yanagi opened the door and called out, 'I've finished.' Mrs Sakura and the twins came in straight away.

'I've tuned it so it sounds the same as before,' Mr Yanagi explained, and Yuni seemed somehow dissatisfied.

'But *we're* not the same as before.' She looked straight in his eyes as she said this.

'I think it's best to have the piano sounding as it was before. If the two of you have changed, you'll produce a tone that's different from how it was in any case.'

Yuni inclined her head slightly, looking uncertain, then turned to me and said, 'What do you think, Mr Tomura?'

'I really don't know.' This was my honest response, and I sensed her look away.

'We won't know unless you play,' Mr Yanagi said. 'Could you try it out for us?'

The twins shared a glance, and then Kazune nodded.

In the past when they'd tested the piano, it was four hands that danced across the keys, two straight backs sitting shoulder to shoulder. Seeing them both in front of the gleaming black instrument was an image that had struck a chord in my heart, even before they had started to play.

Yuni's melodies had been so alluring, gorgeously free-spirited and uninhibited – playing that brought to mind all the most intensely pleasurable joys of life. Kazune's playing, in contrast, was quieter, more subtle. For me it conjured up a mountain spring in the hidden depths of a forest. So what was going to happen now, with only one of them? Would that mountain spring still bubble in its mysterious way?

When Kazune sat down alone at the piano I got a surprise. Her posture was bold and resolute. From the moment she placed her slim fingers on the keyboard and began to play, all memories and worldly thoughts flew away.

It felt as though I'd already been listening to the music before it even began – the melodies, though, I could pick out only here and now. Kazune's presence in this moment was entirely wrapped up in it – it was music that would go on for ever. As I listened to her play, wave after wave washed over me. Her fortitude and strength of character were there for all to hear.

Yuni's cheeks flushed as she watched Kazune from the other side of the piano. Her own capacity to play was long gone, but not Kazune's. I wondered how Yuni was able to endure this, and was brought up short, embarrassed by my concern. More than anyone, it was Yuni who fully believed in the wellspring of her sister's talent.

Kazune stopped playing. She got up from her seat, turned to us and bowed politely.

Instead of returning her bow, I clapped. Yuni, her mother and Mr Yanagi all joined the applause.

'I apologize for having worried you all,' Kazune said. I already knew what she was going to say, even as she drew breath to continue. 'I've decided to start playing again.'

I think she'd already decided a long time ago, only she hadn't noticed it herself. There was no way she could ever leave the piano.

'I want to become a pianist.' A quiet voice, yet one full of determination.

'You mean, you plan to go professional?' Mr Yanagi said.

Kazune's expression finally relaxed and she nodded. 'I do.'

'Very few people make a decent living as a pianist,' Mrs Sakura said quietly. It was obvious as soon as she said it that she hoped her words would go unnoticed. It seemed she couldn't bring herself to say that since only a handful can make it, her daughter should give it all up, yet she couldn't help offering her motherly concern.

'Playing the piano is not how I'll make a living,' Kazune said. 'It's how I'll make a life.'

Her face wore a tranquil smile and her dark eyes were glistening. She struck me then as impossibly beautiful.

I wondered when Kazune had become so strong. I gazed at her in admiration. It was likely something already within her had finally made itself known now that Yuni was no longer able to play. If that was true, then there was a silver lining after all.

Many Routes through the Forest

'IT'S LIKE A JEWEL.' I was a little embarrassed to actually put it into words. 'Like light in a forest . . . I can't really express it properly.'

Mr Yanagi was walking beside me, eyes straight ahead, having completed our tuning at the Sakuras'. 'You're talking about Kazune, I imagine.'

I nodded. More precisely, Kazune's playing – and the way the notes spilled out after another, entwining around each other, generating a scintillating mosaic of sound.

'I'm so happy for her,' he said, and it was evident he truly was thrilled for Kazune.

'Yes, it's wonderful.'

I understood now why they'd asked me to come along. Kazune had wanted to show me her resolve. The confidence she had as she took the very first step. I could almost picture her right foot raised. A small stride with the tip of her toes firmly pointed towards the future, in line with a path that only she could see. And as she lowered her foot, it led straight on to the horizon.

Back when I lived in the mountains I saw something really strange once. It was the same time of year as now and I was returning home from a friend's house one night. I sensed something shining, and on the very edge of the forest saw a tree that was glittering in the darkness. I couldn't understand it and approached timidly to take a closer look.

A wispy light was lodged in the thin branches of an elm tree, twinkling and sparkling. I had no idea what kind of phenomenon might have produced this. It was beautiful – almost frighteningly so – and it wasn't just this one tree. Faint light was glinting on the branches of other nearby trees as well. But that one elm was special, too bright simply to be a reflection of the moonlight. It wasn't ice frozen on the branches, or what mountain people call 'diamond dust' – a cloud of small ice crystals.

Even now I wonder what caused that effect. As I listened to Kazune play, the shimmering glow of the sparkling tree that night filled my mind's eye like some phantom festival.

'I'm so happy for her,' Mr Yanagi said, repeating the sentiment I don't know how many times.

This wasn't a one-off miracle, I was sure of it. The pure beauty of her touch as a pianist wasn't something that just happened. And I knew that trees were sparkling tonight, too, somewhere off in the mountains.

∽

About ten days later the twins came over to the shop, just as we were in the midst of preparing our auditorium for a small weekend recital.

'Wow, this brings back so many memories,' Yuni said excitedly. 'We often used to perform here when we were little.'

They'd both started learning piano as children on our youngsters' piano course.

'Is that the Sakura twins?' Mr Akino said, finishing his tuning and catching sight of the girls.

'It's been so long,' the girls said.

'Look how tall you've grown. Yuni – and Kazune, right? I never used to be able to tell you apart.'

Mr Akino studied each of the twins in turn. Quite some time ago, apparently, Mr Yanagi had taken over tuning the Sakuras' piano in place of Mr Akino. As a rule, we tried to have only one tuner in charge of each piano, but sometimes circumstances would change and a different tuner would take over.

'Since you're here, could we ask you to play something?' Mr Akino asked.

'Are you sure it's OK?' Yuni said, and for a second I thought she might play.

'Of course. I've just finished tuning it. If you don't mind, we'd love to hear you play a piece.'

It was rare for Mr Akino to wear quite such a grin on his face. But then I remembered – he was always charming and easy-going around his clients. And I imagined he was genuinely happy to see the twins after such a long time.

'OK, go ahead,' Yuni said, urging her sister on, and Kazune seated herself in front of the piano.

'Oh, great!' exclaimed Mr Yanagi, who arrived carrying a chair into the room. Putting it down, he hurried over. 'You should have let me know something this exciting was going on,' he said, lightly poking me with an elbow.

'Could you wait a moment?' I said. 'We can't let a rare opportunity like this go by!' I went back to the office and invited Miss Kitagawa to come. 'Would you like to hear Kazune play?' I asked. I wanted everyone in the office – as many people as possible – to hear her.

Miss Kitagawa soon joined me, along with Mr Morohashi, one of our salesmen. By the time I returned with the two extra audience members, Kazune was sitting upright and very still, preparing herself. Lid open, the piano too was waiting with bated breath for its keyboard to be touched by those pale fingers.

There was a sudden intake of breath, then the music began and the piano burst into life. This was a light and charming piece, very different from the one she'd played the other day at home. A lovely, lively piece, recalling for me once again that selfsame tree in the forest, lit up all by itself, glistening on the mountain slopes. It did a great job of showcasing her talents, and I could hardly contain my excited smile. This was not the Kazune we had known in the past. She had never played with such confidence and fluency. The best elements of Yuni's playing seemed to have transferred over to Kazune.

She played the final chord, then rested her hands in her lap, and in that instant of perfect silence, Miss Kitagawa burst into applause. I joined in with enthusiasm.

Kazune stood and bowed. Yuni, beside her, bowed as well.

'That was sublime,' Miss Kitagawa said, a wide smile on her face, still frantically clapping.

From behind her I caught Mr Akino giving a slight nod of approval before he left the small hall.

'Tomura-*kun*.' Our company MD who had joined us silently during the recital came up to me. 'Was she always this good?'

If given a choice between answering *yes* or *no* to this question, I would have gone with *yes*. Kazune's playing had always been remarkable, although today it had something extra. 'It was astonishing – she's totally transformed.'

No, not transformed. Kazune's always been the same Kazune. The seeds were just starting to sprout when I first heard her play, but then they grew rapidly. The stem shot up, leaves spread and the buds finally started to appear. This was just the beginning.

'Of course, she was marvellous before, too,' I said, trying to sound low-key about it, but the boss raised his eyebrows.

'You always were a big supporter of hers, weren't you, Tomura? I feel like she's shown us something extraordinary today, the moment when a person's standard of playing jumps to an altogether higher level. Or maybe it's more like the moment when the person herself develops to the next level. I feel as if we've been witness to that.'

For some reason he wanted to shake my hand. He held it tightly for a moment, patted me on the shoulder and left.

Mr Yanagi went over to congratulate Kazune and returned, looking pleased. 'Wow, she's really something. Really something.'

The twins came over. 'Thank you for everything,' Kazune said. 'Especially since we just showed up without warning.'

Her expression was solemn again, and she bowed to us.

I said, 'Sorry to make you perform for us on the spot like that. You must have come here for a reason.'

'No, we just wanted to say hello and to ask for your continued support. I'm really glad you invited me to play – it's my absolute favourite thing.' Kazune finally broke into a smile.

'Actually . . .' Yuni began, looking right at me. For an instant I was confused. Yuni and Kazune look alike. I knew that. But still – this face. This look. *That's right* – she looked exactly like Kazune did when we'd gone to their house a few days earlier. It was the light in those dark eyes and the flushed cheeks. *She's beautiful*, I couldn't help thinking. Her lips were gently parted, as though holding back words through some giant effort of will.

'I— find I can't give up the piano.'

To give up a precious thing, or not give it up. Was that something you could indeed choose? Or was it more likely that such a thing decided itself?

Yuni's gaze pierced right through me. She said she didn't want to give it up, and yet there was nothing I could do to help her. This was too much for me, but I held her eyes anyway.

'I want to train as a piano tuner.'

There was a silence.

I looked at Yuni's solemn expression and thought: *She isn't giving up the piano at all. There are entrances to the forest all over. And there must be so many routes to walk through it.*

To become a tuner. That, too, was surely one way of walking through the forest. A pianist and a tuner walk through the same forest even though they take different paths.

'I want to tune Kazune's piano.'

'That's—' Mr Yanagi and I spoke at the same time, but I got the distinct feeling we had quite different things to say.

'—very intriguing.' Sure enough, Mr Yanagi completed his thought. 'I know a very good training course. You should study there.'

'Yes, but—' I interrupted, and four dark eyes turned towards me simultaneously.

'But what?' Mr Yanagi was looking at me, too, and I silently shook my head.

Because really my issue was this: *I* wanted to be the one. *I* wanted to tune her piano. But I couldn't say so. I wasn't good enough. I might not make it in time for when Kazune really took flight.

'I think everybody who plays the piano understands this – a pianist stands alone,' Kazune insisted quietly. 'Once you start playing, you're all on your own. That's why I want to play the piano that Yuni has tuned. That's my dream now.'

Her dream. And Yuni's, too.

Mr Yanagi's eyes met mine. 'That's wonderful,' he said.

But I felt frustrated. Is it OK for Yuni to have such a humble dream? Shouldn't she be chasing after something else – some much larger dream, away from her sister's shadow? Kazune was, after all, Kazune, someone who would make a life for herself through the piano.

'Once you start playing, you're all on your own.' Yuni repeated Kazune's words. I could feel the strength of will in her voice. 'So all of us need to do what we can to support her. Like Kazune, I'm going to live for the piano too.'

∽

A SPARKLING TREE IN THE far distant mountains – this image came to me again. Yuni was already determined to become a tuner, that much was clear.

'Thank you for everything today. We'll be going now.' The twins bowed in unison, and as they looked up they both smiled brightly.

I walked them out to the showroom and waved them goodbye. When I returned to the office on the first floor, Mr Yanagi was still pretty worked up.

'I feel like I want to do my very best for them right this minute,' he said. 'I can't remember the last time I felt this way. It's like how I felt when I watched a boxing match on TV. Afterwards I felt all stirred up, like I had to get out and do something ridiculous. Like go for a run.' He sighed and shook his head. 'It's kind of annoying, though. I feel hell-bent on doing my very best, but I don't know what it is I should do my very best at.'

'I feel the same way,' I said.

How could I do my best to help the twins? How could I get better at tuning? If I knew the answer, I would leap into it with every ounce of strength I had. No matter how tough it might be, no matter how painful or trying, I would do it – if only I knew what *it* was.

Perhaps it was the same for a pianist. Learning the basics and practising one's technique are of course indispensable, but how do you polish your expression, your interpretation? It requires an extra unfathomable ingredient to create truly beautiful music. But who can say for certain what that might be or whether it can ever truly be acquired?

'I'm ready to sweat blood here to do my part.' Mr Yanagi, his right hand balled up in a fist, seemed to realize I'd been staring at him all this time. 'Do you know what I mean?'

'I do. Definitely. But I don't know what I should do my best at, or what sort of effort I should make to be able to create a better sound.'

'Ah, so you do understand.' Mr Yanagi looked like he was pondering something. 'Maybe some good, hard physical activity would be the thing for you – early-morning runs, skipping rope. They say swimming's good, too – two kilometres a day in a pool.'

'Do you really think it would help?'

'What do you think?'

My downcast face made him hoot with laughter. 'Building up your strength through running or swimming is important for you as an individual — but it won't really help you develop as a tuner! I wouldn't ever do it myself.'

'You wouldn't?'

'Of course not! I can't stand running. There's something about pounding such filthy roads . . . it's just not for me.'

I smiled, remembering Miss Hamano's words and discoveries of old.

'You spend a lot of time tuning the pianos in the showroom, don't you, Tomura? I think exercise would be about as useful as doing that. I'm not saying that tuning so many pianos of the same brand and in such good condition is a waste of time, but after you've done a few circuits I don't think it's going to be that helpful any more. It's a lot better than not doing it, but it's time to move on to the next level.'

The next level. It's all I wanted — if I was capable of it. But if I didn't do my best I'd only be fooling myself. Kazune and Yuni had already begun to walk their own new paths in life.

A lack of self-confidence was once more rearing its head within me. I felt at a standstill, not knowing how I should proceed. Yet what I wanted more than anything was to spend more time with the twins, to be of service to them as they chased after their dreams.

'How can she make such beautiful chords, like bells ringing in heaven?' I said.

Mr Yanagi grinned.

It was true – everything about her playing was exquisite, but those chords were indescribable. So euphonious that my body felt as if it would melt away, and if I didn't watch myself I'd be in tears. The way she blended the notes was exceptional. I'd heard any number of people play the same piano; why was her tone so unique? What sort of tuning should I do to bring those chords to even greater perfection?

∽

MR YANAGI HAD CLIENTS TO visit, and back at my desk a thought struck me. I wasn't simply imagining that those chords were especially beautiful. Pianos tuned using the equal-tempered system create a slightly dampened, almost muffled sound – was she intentionally playing those sounds with less force? At tuning school I'd studied the theory behind this. A few rare pianists are able to apply a slightly lighter pressure to the keys when playing a chord in order to control the clarity of its sound. As I recalled, musicians of this calibre are also able to employ the pedals with consummate skill to manipulate the resonance.

If Kazune really was one of these exceptional pianists, then what could tuning add? If the pedals were adjusted to be even more responsive, would she still be able to play with such nuance?

I stood up, planning to check the pedals of the piano she'd been playing, but decided not to. The instrument had just been tuned for tomorrow's recital. Fiddling with it now would only spoil that. *Get a grip*, I told myself. But once I sat down I felt the urge again. If I didn't check this now, then I wouldn't be able to try it out the next time Kazune played.

I stood up again and a voice said, 'What's up with you, Tomura-*kun*?' Startled, I fell back on to my seat.

Miss Kitagawa was staring at me with a quizzical look in her eye. 'You've just been bobbing up and down for the last few minutes.'

'I was just – thinking I'd adjust the pedals.'

'Then why don't you?'

'Yeah, but then, maybe it's better not to . . .' I mumbled.

Miss Kitagawa burst out laughing. 'You have something you want to try out, don't you?'

'Well, it's just – when I heard Kazune's chords, I thought that if I adjusted her sustain pedal so it's a touch more sensitive, it might make it easier for her to play. It's just an idea.'

'Then you should just go for it.'

I hastily shook my head. 'No, I don't know if it would be helpful or not. It might be totally unnecessary.'

Again Miss Kitagawa chuckled. 'Listen, Tomura-*kun*. That idea of yours could be helpful to her, or maybe it won't. Even if it isn't, it might turn out to be useful to your tuning technique in the future.'

'Miss Kitagawa . . . when I first heard Mr Itadori tuning a piano, it changed my life.'

'Wow.' She smiled knowingly.

'I don't know if music is *useful* to my life as such, but that's when my inner life really began. It was an experience that went way beyond being useful or not.'

'I understand.' Miss Kitagawa gave a decisive nod. 'Which is why I think you should act on your idea. If it doesn't work out, you go back to where you started. But it might help Kazune.'

I'd been sitting down, but stood up once again.

'Listening to you, Tomura-*kun*, reminds me of a murder mystery I read a long time ago.'

'What do you mean?'

Miss Kitagawa stood up, walked over to me, and said in a low voice, 'The plot of the book was really interesting, but the solution at the end was – how should I put it? – a little unusual. When the criminal phoned the protagonist he didn't say a word but there was a faint *thump, thump* in the background.'

Where was she going with this?

'When the protagonist heard the sound he knew where the call was coming from. The criminal had a small dog and that dog, on its last legs, was lying on its side, its tail beating listlessly on the floor. That small sound gave him away.' Miss Kitagawa let out a breath. 'From the tiniest, most trivial-seeming of clues, you might discover how to draw out the most beautiful sounds from a piano. The conclusion could turn out to be wrong, or a red herring. But seeing whether it can be done or not is the mark of a tuner with flair.'

I shifted awkwardly in my seat.

'I believe you can do it. My guess is you're good at discovering those tiny clues, but your technical skills may not be quite up to it yet.'

I knew that the kind Miss Kitagawa was doing her best to encourage me.

∽

THE ROAD AHEAD WAS STEEP and long, and I had no firm idea as to how to achieve my goals. First came the will to do it, then persistence and effort. And then maybe something else entirely.

Working with pianos every day. Paying careful attention to what clients might tell me. Polishing my tuning instruments. Retuning the pianos in our showroom, one by one. Listening to piano music, advice from Mr Akino and Mr Yanagi, hints from Mr Itadori. Kazune's rich and wonderful melodies.

And maybe, during our short summer, lying down with the scent of grass all around, seeing the trees glowing at night in the mountains, listening closely to the murmur of a mountain spring as it bubbles out of the ground.

The spinning needle of my inner compass had now come to a halt. All the red arrows hovering over so many different pianos – in the forest, in town, in the gym of my sixth-form college – all of them were now pointing in a single direction. Towards Kazune's piano.

Tune for the Individual

KAZUNE'S WORDS, 'THE PIANO is how I'll make a life,' kept replaying in my head, along with her wilful, commanding tone as she said them. Her flushed cheeks. Her dark, sparkling eyes.

In the mornings as I walked to work I mulled this over and over. Kazune's playing, her words, her expression. I knew these weren't just meant for me, but even so they moved me. Even in my lowly state there had to be some way I could give something back to her. Some response I could offer.

I unlocked the door to the deserted office. When I'd first started with the company I'd assumed that as the new boy I would open up in the morning. But I was soon told not to worry about that. Mr Akino came to work early because the roads weren't so busy then, so I needn't concern myself with opening the shop up.

This morning, however, I couldn't contain myself. I couldn't wait to get to the office and get my hands on a piano.

It wasn't just because she was so skilled that I liked Kazune's playing. There was something beyond the beautiful and refined depths of her tone – an anticipatory tension that something was about to be revealed.

That extra something in Kazune's playing was no lingering shadow, nor was there any sense of her having taken on the burden of playing on behalf of a bitter and regretful Yuni, whose own dreams of life as a pianist had come to an abrupt end. Kazune had digested all of this, and out of it had been born an altogether fresh, new radiance.

∽

BACK IN THE OFFICE I flung open all the windows. Morning light flooded the rooms, and the early breeze still contained a residual coolness.

I imagined how, for Kazune, from the moment she decided to become a professional pianist, the world must have looked so different to her. I'd been the same age then as Kazune was now: seventeen when I encountered Mr Itadori. And I could still recall the ecstasy I'd felt when I decided to become a tuner. Nothing was for certain, yet I was full of elation as though the mist before my eyes had suddenly cleared, and for the first time my feet were properly touching the ground as I walked; a deep happiness so palpable I could almost trace its outline. Right at that moment, I was sure I could walk as far as I would ever need to.

On the day we started tuning the Sakuras' piano again, the twins' mother told me Kazune never found practising the piano a strain, however long she sat at the keyboard.

'She says she never gets tired, no matter how long she plays,' Mrs Sakura said, smiling sweetly.

'Being able to play that long is a talent in itself,' Mr Yanagi put in.

And I totally agreed. It wasn't as if Kazune was forcing herself to play. Someone who can put in hard graft without resentment is at a distinct advantage. If you find something difficult or boring, you're more likely to want a major return on your investment of time and effort and then be dissatisfied with the outcome. But because Kazune was able to slog away at her practice and enjoy it, the possibilities before her were beyond imagining.

There was a decisiveness to how she approached the piano that I envied. Seated at the keyboard, it seemed she was capable of almost anything.

Personally, I didn't know where to focus my efforts, which is why I did things in such a haphazard manner. But there in the office at that early hour, I opened up the lid of a grand piano (the same model as the one in Kazune's home) and set myself a clear goal: to retune this one instrument using the well-tempered system.

When tuning a piano there are several schemes available for dealing with the twelve musical intervals of an octave – the do, re, mi, fa, so, la, ti, do, plus the semitones. The two main methods are well-tempered and equal-tempered tuning.

Equal-tempered is a system based on logic, dividing an octave into twelve equal parts, and is the tuning used for nearly all pianos. There are a few issues with it, since adjacent notes are tuned to have an equal interval between them even though, strictly speaking, they are not a regular distance apart in terms of resonance, so when you combine sounds they result in a certain muddiness. For instance, with chords, the *mi* notes in do-mi-so and in la-do-mi are intrinsically different pitches.

By contrast, well-tempered tuning prioritizes this resonance of sounds. It regulates things so that the frequency of each note is a ratio of whole numbers in mathematical terms. When you put several sounds together, the simpler the frequency ratio, the more the resonance is pleasing to the ear – which is why chords sound so beautiful on a piano tuned to the well-tempered system. There is one significant weakness to this method, however, namely that since the interval between each note is different, it can't be used when you change key.

With a string or wind instrument a player can modify the pitch of notes himself. With the minor chord do-mi-so, for instance, if the *mi* is flat it can be tweaked upwards a little to create a perfect harmony. But in order to do that a player has to fully grasp the tonality of the *mi*, what chord it's in and its precise location in the chord sequence. Also, the player needs the technical ability to discern all that from the instrument while he continues to play. I understood the theory behind it all, but knew as well that very few musicians could reach this level of skill.

On the piano this is impossible. There is a fixed sequence of sounds and a player is unable to modify the musical intervals himself. He has to play within the pattern of sound we tuners have created. If he senses a slight lack of sparkle to the harmony, all he can do is live with it as he plays.

So I was keen to try well-tempered tuning in spite of misgivings about my ability. But nothing is *absolute*. 'Correct', 'useful', 'wasted' – these words are neither helpful nor true. I simply wanted to learn and was keen to give well-tempered tuning a try.

It took me under an hour to retune the piano from equal-tempered to well-tempered, and I was excited to hear the difference in tone. As I couldn't play the piano myself, I just pressed the keys to see how they resonated. Do-mi-so, so-ti-re, fa-la-do. I'd have to retune it back to equal-tempered tuning before the end of the day and regretted this deeply, since the new sound was exquisite.

'What's going on in here?' It was Mr Itadori, looking in from the door to the showroom. 'Oh, it's you, Tomura-*kun*.' He bent backwards in mock surprise. 'What have you been doing here?'

I couldn't understand what he meant.

'It's so much better all of a sudden.'

'What is?'

'Your tuning, of course.' His tone was even, his expression quite serious. 'You've achieved such a superb clarity of sound.'

It made me really happy to hear that. But it couldn't be true. I'd changed the tuning to well-tempered, but timbre and tone? I hadn't intentionally worked on those.

'Very nice,' Mr Itadori said, a smile stretching from ear to ear.

'Thank you very much.'

Still beaming, Mr Itadori exited the room.

Was he right? Was my tuning really improving? I wiped the keyboard with a cloth and gently closed the lid.

Mr Yanagi had used a restaurant metaphor once. He'd described how a chef, since he doesn't know who is going to eat the dish, will go to great lengths to make sure anyone tasting it will be delighted from the very first bite. But if you do know who is going to eat it, you can target that person's preferences and give them the flavours they prefer. Tuning is the same. If you know the person who will play the piano, you can tune it to produce the optimal sound for them, with the whole palette of tonal colours that particular person most wants in their instrument.

A SINGLE MAGPIE FLUTTERS IN *and comes to rest in a forest of* spruce.

I tuned the piano in the showroom with Kazune's playing in mind, doing it for the sake of the piano that she would play, now that she had decided to turn professional.

It Only Takes Ten Thousand

From that day, I started going out on increasing numbers of tuning jobs on my own, and gradually gathered a number of repeat customers.

I grew familiar with the homes I visited. Not the houses so much or the clients, but the pianos. *Oh*, I'd think. I'd open up the black lid and see clear traces of a previous tuning I'd done. It felt like staring at my reflection in a mirror. What I'd had in mind, what I'd been aiming for, what I'd accomplished. I was amazed how I could see it all, reflected back.

I'm not that sociable or friendly, but with a piano I could feel a closeness I lacked with people. *How have you been?* I wanted to say aloud. *It's been a while.* That I felt that way made sense, since a part of me remained behind within each piano.

Sometimes it felt as if a piano that had been all prim and stiff a year earlier, was now opening up a little, drawing closer to me, and the same held true for the clients. Those who had stuck close by on my previous visit, watching my every move as I worked, now left me to my own devices.

'All thanks to you, I now regard my piano as a very fine instrument indeed.' This came from an elderly lady whose piano I had tuned on one of my first appointments of the day. 'It makes me so happy to see how carefully, how lovingly, you treat it,' she added.

I felt a little embarrassed. 'No, please, I should thank *you* for allowing me to work on it,' I told her.

She wasn't praising the sound I'd created, but at this point in my career any words of praise still felt wholly unmerited.

That isn't to say I didn't enjoy hearing them. I loaded my tools into the little car and drove back to the office quite full of myself.

Mr Yanagi was just leaving the shop as I arrived. 'What's up? You seem in a good mood,' he said. Mr Yanagi seemed pretty cheerful himself.

'I was thinking how blessed I am to have such wonderful clients.'

'Clients, eh?'

I thought about it then added, 'And such brilliant mentors, too.'

Mr Yanagi glanced at me, chuckling. 'Hey, you don't have to worry about sucking up to me! I was just thinking how very like you that is – that you reckon you're blessed with wonderful clients.'

'Really?'

'Don't take this the wrong way,' he prefaced, and his next words hit me hard, 'but you're not blessed with anything special.'

He was right. Of course he was right.

'At most, some good clients, some good mentors – that's about it.'

I didn't have a particularly good ear, wasn't that clever with my hands, and had no grounding in music. So I wasn't blessed in any way at all. I had nothing. I was only here because of my obsession with that big, black instrument.

'What I mean is, it's all based on your own technical know-how, Tomura.'

'Hmm?'

Mr Yanagi grinned. 'It's not that you're blessed with wonderful clients – it's your own ability that gets you the jobs.'

I couldn't come up with an immediate response, and watched in silence as he walked out.

I felt like I'd just been hit over the head.

'But how does one become a *great* tuner?'

I must have said this out loud as I returned to my desk, because a voice answered from behind me.

'First you have to put in ten thousand hours.'

I turned and saw Miss Kitagawa looking at me.

'They say that if you put in ten thousand hours towards any goal, things will fall into place. If you're going to worry, best to wait until after you've done your ten thousand hours and then see.'

I calculated how many days that would come to. 'About five or six years, isn't it?'

She held up a calculator from her desk to show me her own workings. 'You can't spend every minute of every day tuning, plus you need days off.'

I scanned across to Mr Akino, busy with his paperwork. 'Mr Akino?' I said, but got no response. 'Mr Akino, could I go out with you again to watch you tune?'

Slowly he withdrew the earplug from his left ear. 'I'm busy. How about getting Mr Itadori to let you watch him, instead of me?' He presented this in a disinterested monotone, without even looking up.

'I'd really appreciate that, too. I, er . . .' I hesitated. 'The thing is, I'm not planning to become a concert piano tuner, but I want to get good at tuning domestic pianos.'

He let out a long sigh. 'I see. Yeah, you've got to start there.' He rubbed his eyes and then lowered his voice. 'But are you sure that's all you want? She's going to be performing recitals before long.'

It took three seconds for it to click with me that *she* meant Kazune. Before long she would be performing recitals – Mr Akino had said it so casually it took me by surprise. It made me so happy that Mr Akino, with his keen sense of hearing, recognized Kazune's talent.

'Mr Itadori does ordinary domestic piano tuning, too. He does a pretty amazing job with that as well.'

'Amazing how?'

'Why don't you go and check it out yourself?' Mr Akino said, sounding a little exasperated. 'It's reborn.'

'What is?'

'The piano. It's reborn into something totally different.'

Mr Akino pulled a very strange face when he said this, almost as if what he was about to say was something he didn't comprehend himself.

'When Mr Itadori tunes your piano it makes you wonder what the piano was up to until then. You can't believe what a great sound it's suddenly making – you feel like your playing has suddenly improved.'

How wonderful is that? What a lucky piano. *Both* people need to feel satisfied – the person who plays that piano, and the tuner himself who can make someone so happy.

Mr Akino sighed again. 'Tomura, do you understand what I mean by the piano's *touch*? You probably think of it as the keyboard having a light or a heavy feel when you press the notes, yes? Actually it's not so simple. When you press a key with your finger it connects to a hammer, which strikes a string. I'm talking about that sensation. A pianist doesn't sound the keyboard. He strikes a string. It's possible to play in such a way that you feel your fingertips connect directly with the hammers and with those hammers striking the strings. That feeling is the special touch Mr Itadori has.'

'That's extraordinary. I would think everyone who plays would ask Mr Itadori to tune for them, if they knew that.'

Mr Akino ignored my gushing admiration. 'Treat the piano with high reverence. It can teach you all manner of things.'

I took this to be Mr Akino's way of saying how wonderful the instrument is.

'What do you mean by "all manner of things"?'

It was an honest question, but Mr Akino kept his eyes lowered for a while.

'When a pianist plays the piano,' he said, 'he expresses everything in his imagination through the tone of his music. To switch it around, a pianist is unable to play any sound that does not already exist within him – but the piano enables his skill and technique to come out loud and clear.' Mr Akino stared at me now, his expression unusually grave. He stuffed the earplug back in his left ear, indicating the end of the conversation.

I understood him to mean that Mr Itadori's tuning was to be revered. Truly, his gift was to arrange the soundscape of a piano so that its music would shine light into the shadows, revealing even those things that would rather remain out of sight.

Perhaps it was a piano tuned by Mr Itadori that had led Mr Akino himself to give up on his dreams of a career as a pianist. Possibly Mr Akino imagined that Mr Itadori had done this intentionally.

I viewed Mr Itadori as the ideal, the kind of tuner I wanted to become, but Mr Akino must have viewed him through different eyes.

The Answer Is in the Stars

POLISHING MY TUNING HAMMER, I sat at my desk in the office waiting for my next appointment.

'Here you are,' Miss Kitagawa said, placing a cup of tea on my desk.

'Oh, thank you very much.'

Miss Kitagawa watched intently as I folded up the cloth I'd been using to polish the tuning hammer and set it aside.

'Your tuning tools always look so immaculate, Tomura-*kun*.' She seemed genuinely impressed. 'You've been here two years now?'

'That's right.' I would soon be starting my third year. The tuning hammer she was admiring was the seasoned tool Mr Itadori had given me all that time ago.

'When you first came here, Tomura-*kun*, and I heard you were born and raised in the mountains, it made sense to me. You seemed selfless, gentle, straightforward, and for better or for worse, the sort of person who doesn't stand out. You didn't strike me as the cheerful type either. I couldn't picture what kind of work you'd do here as a tuner since you don't seem to show a strong preference for anything, one way or the other.'

No strong preference – she was right about that. When I arrived in town to attend sixth-form college I realized for the first time that I'd never had any strong likes or dislikes about anything at all. My peers seemed to know about all kinds of things and had strong opinions about them. I alone was non-committal. In the mountains, the information and knowledge we could get hold of was limited. Compared to the town, living there took a lot more time and effort, and there were probably many aspects of that life that made us less picky about every little thing.

Inside I hadn't changed. Other than the sound of the piano, I really didn't have strong feelings about anything, one way or the other.

'But you know,' Miss Kitagawa continued, 'you still come in here early every morning and wipe down everyone else's desk, don't you? And not just a simple once-over, but a thorough clean. I don't know for sure, but I rather get the feeling that life in the mountains must be like that – that's to say, if you don't do things the right way it could be dangerous. So if you don't bundle up you could freeze to death, or if you don't take proper precautions you could get attacked by some wild animal or something.'

'It's not like that, not really.'

'Keep your tuning hammer neatly polished at all times, yes? I get the feeling that you've had it drummed into you that you need to take good care of your tools, or else when you really need them they won't work and your life could be in danger.'

I didn't know what to say.

'You're really putting him on the spot.'

I heard a suppressed chuckle and turned to see Mr Akino wiping his hands on a handkerchief and heading back to his desk.

'Miss Kitagawa, you're being weird,' he said. 'You are most definitely making Tomura uncomfortable.'

Miss Kitagawa gave a little pout and said in a low voice, 'Tomura-*kun*, people know you're doing your best. Don't let it get to you.'

Tray in hand, she returned to her desk.

'What was the old bat comforting you about?'

I didn't think Miss Kitagawa was that old, but Mr Akino resumed speaking before I could correct him.

'Has one of your clients requested a different tuner?'

I nodded vaguely. I didn't think I'd done anything wrong, but indeed another of my clients had requested that someone else be put in charge of tuning their piano.

'I didn't know what to do.' I hesitated, then went ahead and explained what had happened at a home I'd visited the previous day. 'After I'd finished tuning and testing the piano, the client asked me if this was the absolute best possible sound.'

The client had told me that he'd decided to have the piano tuned after a long period of neglect because his grandchild, now entering primary school, would soon be starting piano lessons. The instrument was in bad shape, but I'd cleaned it inside and got it all back in tune.

'He wanted his grandchild to be trained to appreciate the arts, using a piano offering the best sound possible.'

Mr Akino grunted.

'When he asked me if this was the absolute best sound, I just couldn't say yes.'

There's no such thing as an absolute best sound. No sound is absolute. It would have been better if I'd said it was, but I couldn't. For a child being pushed to have an appreciation for the arts, hearing adults insist this was the absolute best possible sound was not going to help.

'You're quite the fool, Tomura.' Mr Akino sounded pleased with himself. 'You should have just agreed. No one likes to play the piano if they have concerns over whether or not it has a good sound.'

'I suppose so.'

I nodded briefly, but then hung my head in doubt.

'Isn't it enough if a client thinks it sounds good?' I said. 'I don't know – I just don't like the idea of someone else deciding whether it's the absolute best sound or not.'

Mr Akino gave a small, dry laugh. 'You can be such a pain, Tomura.'

I'm a pain. Is that why people want to switch to a different tuner?

∽

WHEN I LIVED IN THE mountains the doctor would visit our local clinic on Mondays and Thursdays only. He made very clear diagnoses and did not mince his words. He'd diagnose a cold as a cold. 'You're going to be fine,' he'd declare in some cases, while in others he'd caution patients about their prospects in no uncertain terms. After I moved away from the mountains, I never saw another doctor who spoke quite so plainly or conclusively.

Which approach is the more honest? Perhaps the one found in town hospitals, where doctors will consider a range of possibilities. But is avoiding a definite diagnosis really helpful to the patient, or is it just a way for doctors to shirk their responsibility? I started to have my doubts. I remembered how this felt.

'So how did you answer him?'

'I told him if you're going to use the word "absolute", then I don't think this is the *absolute* best sound.'

'You weren't wrong and you didn't lie.' Mr Akino cocked his head to one side to ponder the question. 'If you're going to respond as honestly as you can, then sure, you might answer in that way. But if you do, it sounds more like your subjective opinion.'

Unless you have a relationship built on trust, a subjective approach won't be of any interest to the other person. But that's what I didn't understand — how to establish that kind of mutual trust.

'Even if you can't explain it in words, if you tune it so it sounds good, that's enough,' Mr Akino said. 'Putting aside the question of absolutes, the end game is to make it sound good.'

Fair enough. But what had me in knots was the question of how to go about creating that gorgeous sound in the first place.

'Back in ancient Greece,' Mr Akino began, twirling a pen around his index finger, 'learning was divided into two areas — astronomy and music. In other words, if you studied both astronomy and music you could shine a light on anything in the world. That's what they believed back then.'

'I see.'

'Music was one part of the twin foundations, Tomura.'

So in ancient Greece they saw the world as being constructed from astronomy and music. That sounds like a splendid world to live in, although my memory of ancient Greece was that they were fighting battles with each other all the time.

'Do you know how many constellations there are?'

I shook my head and Mr Akino gave a triumphant little smirk.

'That would be eighty-eight.'

Now that he mentioned it, I remembered thinking it was strange when we studied the constellations in science at school. You could connect up the prominent stars, see them as forming a shape and name them. But scattered among them were other smaller stars you could also make out with the naked eye. You couldn't just ignore them and come up with those other shapes, could you? It was pretty outrageous to settle on only eighty-eight constellations out of all the countless stars in the sky, infinite as the grains of sand by the sea or in the endless deserts of our planet.

In a way, though, I could see how astronomy and music could be considered fundamental to understanding the world. You extract some stars from all the countless ones and make them into constellations. Tuning is similar. You select things of beauty that have dissolved into the fabric of the world. You gingerly extract that beauty, careful not to damage it, and then you make it visible.

Seven sounds – do, re, mi, fa, so, la, ti, do, or twelve if you include semitones – are teased out, named, and then they sparkle just like the constellations. And it's the tuner's job to pick these out with precision from the vast ocean of sound, arrange them delicately and make them resonate.

'Tomura-*kun*! Are you listening?' Head in hands, Mr Akino stared at me across the desk, looking somewhat put out. 'The number of constellations: eighty-eight. It's the same number as the keys on a piano.'

'Ohh.'

'A legacy from the twin pillars of Greek civilization, astronomy and music.'

'Now hold it right there, Mr Akino.' Miss Kitagawa interrupted him, seemingly unable to let that comment pass by unremarked. 'Don't you go spouting any more of your nonsense. Tomura-*kun* will start to believe you.'

'Nonsense?' Mr Akino shrugged and looked away.

Which part was nonsense? I'd learned the history of the piano back in tuning school. It developed from the earlier harpsichord. Its keyboard did not have eighty-eight keys. And there was not even a prototype of the harpsichord back in ancient Greece. It was in Beethoven's time, about two hundred years ago, that the piano replaced the harpsichord. At first it had anywhere from sixty-eight to seventy-three keys. Beethoven's 'Moonlight Sonata' has the inscription *For harpsichord or piano*. People believe that Beethoven changed his primary instrument from the harpsichord to the piano only between composing the first and second movements. It was at this time that the keyboard became fixed at eighty-eight keys.

Was eighty-eight really the number of the constellations? Or was the point about astronomy and music being the first fields of study itself a bit of nonsense? I didn't know any of the facts, but went ahead and opened my notebook anyway. The number of constellations, the number of keys. As I wrote down *eighty-eight*, I noticed Mr Akino leaning across the desk towards me.

'So you're still taking notes, eh?' He peered into my notebook, and I hastily snapped it shut.

I was embarrassed. I was about to start my third year as a tuner, yet was still noting down basic information like a rank amateur.

'I think that's fine,' Mr Akino said blandly. 'Sometimes I wish I'd been as diligent at taking notes as you. When you first start a job you see and hear all kinds of important things. If only I'd taken notes I might have made faster progress. It wasn't so much that I disliked the time and effort required, but rather that I was operating under a misconception. I figured mastering technique meant learning it through your body.' He stared at the closed notebook and added, 'It's an illusion. The idea that your ears will remember, your fingers will learn – it's all an illusion. *This* is what remembers it all.' Mr Akino pointed an index finger at his head.

So it wasn't just me. I'd also been sure that you learned technique physically, through your body. So much time passing and still being unable to master the essentials made me half give up, figuring I just didn't have a musical physique. I continued to take notes, not wanting to waste any time gnashing my teeth.

'You can't just write it down, though,' Mr Akino said. 'You have to remember it. It's like memorizing historical dates. At some point you'll suddenly grasp the big picture.'

Of course you can't express everything about tuning in words. Not even one-hundredth, or one-thousandth of it. I know that, so I don't rely on words alone. But the process of translating the techniques of tuning into words has allowed me to tether the music that would otherwise flow right on by, pinning my body to each and every technique I was trying to master.

'So what's with the big discussion?' Mr Yanagi said as he cheerily swept into the room.

'Nothing special. We were just talking about how terrible the weather is,' Mr Akino said brusquely.

'It really *is* terrible weather. A good rainstorm like this will completely mess up a tuning— Oh!'

At this *Oh*, everyone turned to look at Mr Yanagi.

'I – I have something to announce.' Mr Yanagi lightly cleared his throat. 'I'm, er – getting married soon.'

'Really? For sure this time?' I asked.

'Yep, this time for sure.' Mr Yanagi was beaming with joy. He'd been saying for ever that he was going to get married. Miss Hamano had kept delaying, saying she had some big work project she had to attend to. She apparently did translations – maybe the book she was working on was finally getting published.

'Congrats.'

'Congratulations!'

'Thank you, thank you.'

Mr Yanagi was all smiles, not even trying to hide his happiness.

I don't know if marriage is such a great thing or not, but it did feel good to see him looking this ecstatic. I didn't think to add something like *I wish you all the best*, and ended up just gazing at him in silence.

∽

BAG OF TUNING TOOLS IN hand, I headed out on my way. The rain had let up, and the wind, which had been cold enough to sting my cheeks, had dropped. Patches of blue were appearing in the sky. Spring was just around the corner.

Mr Yanagi was climbing out of his car. 'Thought it was about time to put on regular tyres.'

'I suppose so.'

'Oh, by the way, I meant to say: keep the second Sunday in May free.'

'OK.'

'We're holding the reception at a restaurant after the wedding ceremony that day.'

'Lovely! I've never been to a wedding before.'

'I guess you're too young to have had many friends you know get married yet.'

I couldn't think of anybody, even a few years down the road, who would be likely to invite me to a wedding reception. Maybe my younger brother.

'One other thing – do you have a minute?'

I nodded and placed my heavy bag on the ground. I'd started out early so I still had plenty of time.

'I was thinking of having some entertainment at the party.'

'I see.'

'I was going to invite my band, but punk rock and a wedding reception aren't exactly a good fit, so we're going to have a piano instead.'

'That's a great idea!'

'I found a couple of restaurants with pianos. A restaurant with a nice instrument but so-so food, or one with fantastic food but only a so-so piano – which would you choose?'

'The one with the good piano.'

'I agree!' Mr Yanagi looked down at his bag of tuning tools. 'But she wanted to go for the one that has the best food.'

'Ah.'

That was a little surprising. I would have thought Miss Hamano would go with the piano.

'The food I can leave up to others, but she told me, "The piano you should be able to take care of, Yanagi."'

'Really?'

'No *reallys* about it. The groom is very busy on his special day. If I weren't the groom I'd do my best with the piano, but I'm going to have my hands full. So I was thinking . . .' Mr Yanagi held my eyes. 'I asked a very good pianist to play for us.'

'That's wonderful.'

'Work-related guests with a good ear for music will be coming. But whether or not the guests have a good enough ear, or have even heard a decent pianist, listening to a wonderful recital while dining is a perfect way to celebrate.'

He looked so happy it made me happy too.

'I was thinking of having you tune the piano, Tomura.'

This came so out of the blue, my voice shot up an octave:

'But – th–there must be someone else you could—?'

Mr Akino would be good, and naturally Mr Itadori would be superb.

'I'd like you to do it, if you're OK with that?'

For a moment I questioned whether I should accept, me being a junior tuner and all. This was a very special day for them. It would be better to have someone more skilled than me to do the tuning.

'The pianist is going to be Kazune-*chan*.'

'Wha—?'

I was astonished. What a wonderful party that would be – to dine while listening to Kazune play the piano.

'You'd like to do the tuning now, I bet.' Mr Yanagi grinned.

'No— I think—'

All the more reason to have someone better than me do the tuning, I was about to say, when an emotion I couldn't suppress welled up in me.

'I can do it,' I announced, in a voice so decisive it took me by surprise. 'Please let me do it.'

I bowed my head, and Mr Yanagi nodded in delight.

V

A MASTER CLASS

Greatness =
Perseverance + Resignation

THAT EVENING WHEN I got back to the office there was a message taped to my desk.

Tomorrow's appointment with Mr Kimura is cancelled.

Cancelled? I had a bad feeling about this. I went over to check the details with Miss Kitagawa, who'd taken the call. 'He's not rescheduling for later, but cancelling altogether?'

Miss Kitagawa shifted uncomfortably in her seat.

'Another one who wants to change tuners?'

'Umm,' she said, avoiding my eyes.

'Did he not want us to handle his tuning in the future at all?'

'No, he didn't go that far.'

'I'm really sorry,' I said, and bowed my head. I sensed all eyes in the office on me.

'There's no need for you to apologize, Tomura-*kun*. It's not like he said he's changing companies because he doesn't like you. It's possible he simply isn't playing the piano any more.'

If that was the case, he would have said so.

'At any rate, it's not your fault. Times are tough all round. There aren't that many families who play the piano as a hobby and have the extra cash to get them tuned regularly every year.'

She managed to make it sound as if it wasn't my fault at all. But that couldn't be. If he'd been pleased with my tuning, I'm sure he wouldn't have cancelled.

Returning to my desk, I was careful not to let my feelings show, but was unable to hold back an enormous sigh. *Am I really that bad?* I happened to glance up and saw Mr Akino look away quickly.

'What do you think is the single most important thing for a tuner?' I ventured to ask.

Mr Akino, still not looking at me, said, 'A good tuning hammer.'

'No, that isn't what I meant,' I said, pressing him, when a voice from the other side of the office chipped in, 'Perseverance.'

This came from Mr Yanagi. 'And courage, too.'

'Plus resignation,' Mr Akino muttered.

All kinds of responses were flying at me. They didn't say anything about *talent* or *ability*, and for that, with the way I was feeling now, I felt incredibly grateful.

'Perseverance I suppose I can understand,' Miss Kitagawa said with a wry laugh.

I could understand courage, too. You can completely change the nature of a piano with your ministrations – without courage you could never take on that responsibility. 'Then what about resignation?' All eyes turned to Mr Akino.

'Come on, guys, I think you're misunderstanding me.' Mr Akino pulled a long face. 'No matter what you do,' he said, 'you'll never reach perfection. At a certain point you have to come to a decision, say this is it, put your tools down and give up.'

'And if you don't, then what?' Mr Yanagi asked the question that was already on my lips.

'If you can never decide when to call it quits, then at some point you go mad,' Mr Akino said lightly.

I wondered if the silence in the room meant they all agreed. Pursue perfection, refuse to give up and you're on the route to insanity. Had I ever been in danger of that myself, even for a moment?

'Didn't we talk about this once before?' Mr Yanagi asked.

'Well, we talked about why Tomura might have clients cancel on him or ask to change tuners,' Mr Akino said.

'I don't think that Tomura's made any major slip-ups. I remember bringing up the idea about the ten thousand hours,' Miss Kitagawa said.

'No one really accepts that notion,' Mr Akino said.

Ah, so *that's* it. The theory that people had no faith in me because I was young and inexperienced was simply offered as a consolation.

'People who can do the work manage it even if they haven't put in ten thousand hours. And those who can't, can't, even with countless hours under their belt.'

Mr Yanagi gazed up at the ceiling. 'That's a pretty blunt way of putting it.'

'Everybody knows it, they just don't say it. So it's not worth thinking about ability or aptitude because it won't get you anywhere if you do.'

A pause, then Mr Akino added, 'You just do the work.'

That sent a chill up my spine. Was that true of Mr Akino too?

'You can live without talent. But in our hearts we still believe that something we can't quite grasp even after ten thousand hours will somehow, maybe, all fall into place after twenty thousand. Isn't it more important to build up a higher, broader view than to try to see things too simplistically?'

'Yes,' I said, my voice hoarse. I didn't want to agree so readily. I wasn't sure if I really got it, but I did think that what he said was, for the most part, true. We're not here and surviving because we have talent. Whether you have it or not, you keep on living. And I didn't want to agonize over whether I had it or not. The only option was to do the work and discover with my own hands something substantial, something meaningful.

'Hi, everyone, I'm back,' rang a reassuring voice from the door. Mr Itadori was just coming back into the office.

Before I could say anything, Mr Yanagi asked, 'Mr Itadori, what do you consider to be the single most important asset for a tuner?'

As he placed his tuning bag on the floor, he replied, in his gentle voice, 'That would be the clients.'

I recalled the sublime tone Mr Itadori had created in the concert hall to support the performance of the top-flight pianist. Yet without a doubt it was the pianist himself – Mr Itadori's client, in other words – who had succeeded in drawing that sound from the piano, with Mr Itadori's assistance.

And what about me? I wondered. My clients' faces came to me. A smiling, nodding face; a sullen, unhappy one. Even the faces of those clients whose names I couldn't recall immediately rose up in my mind's eye, one after the other. It was true: the ones who had trained me were – no doubt about it – my clients. Kazune's solemn face now appeared to me, but as soon as it did I saw her break into a smile.

A True Master
Is Forever a Pupil

THE DAY BEFORE THE wedding I arrived to tune the piano at the restaurant where the reception was to be held. The ambience of the place was warm and inviting, with the grand piano installed in one corner of the attractive dining area.

It was a finer class of piano than I'd been expecting, since Mr Yanagi had told me they'd prioritized food over the quality of the instrument. Keeping my excitement in check, I opened up the fallboard – only for my heart to plummet to my boots the moment I laid eyes on the keyboard. A closer inspection was enough to confirm my worst fears. The height of the keys was misaligned by about 0.5 mm, some higher, some lower. I tapped on a few notes and found my misgivings were justified. The sound was all over the place.

I pictured Kazune playing it. Seated at this piano in her sixth-form-college uniform, she would do her level best – although would she even be wearing her uniform to a wedding reception? Probably not, yet I couldn't imagine her wearing anything else. I pictured her playing, her posture erect, delicately running her fingers up and down the keyboard. And the sounds she would create flowed like water from a cool, clear spring into my ears.

I struck a few more notes on the piano in front of me. No, this was in no way fit for Kazune – I didn't want to make her play this as it was. So keeping her constantly in mind, I set about tuning the instrument.

I lifted and propped open the lid. It still moves me every single time I see the tuning pins all neatly arranged inside, like so many trees in the forest. The soundboard made of spruce sends pulses of vibration racing out at thousands of metres per second. This was where I would help create Kazune's sound. This was where I would neatly part the undergrowth to make it easier for her to enter the forest.

I started by adjusting the keys so that they were uniform in height. The cushion connecting each one to the keyboard had completely worn out on the inside. Here I inserted very thin slivers of paper to adjust the height. The normal movable range of a key, depressing it from its full height to the base, is only some 10 mm, so a difference of even 0.5 mm would make it awfully hard to play. After equalizing the height I turned my attention to the depth, and I pressed each note in turn, checking the position where it struck the strings.

Only then did I begin the actual tuning process. I'd discussed this in advance with Mr Yanagi, who had told me to close my eyes when I decided on the sound I wanted. I didn't think this was just another metaphor. I closed my eyes, listened intently, fixed the idea in my mind of each sound that welled up, and adjusted each tuning pin accordingly.

I worked outside the regular flow of time and space, my senses on full alert, my concentration unwavering. Once I had finished, I realized that nearly four hours had gone by. The piano was much improved now, I thought.

KAZUNE'S REHEARSAL WAS SET FOR early on the morning of the reception so that in the event of a problem, I'd have enough time to put it right.

'I'm so happy, because I wanted to get used to playing this piano as soon as I could,' Kazune said. 'The piano at home, the one at school, pianos at performances and competitions – each and every one has its own personality.' She said this while pulling her sheet music from a bag.

Yuni nodded beside her. 'I always found our piano at home the easiest one to play,' she said. 'But when I played a concert grand in an auditorium for the first time, I was just blown away.'

That just had to be a piano tuned by Mr Itadori, I was sure of it.

'Well, it had a great sound and was surprisingly easy to play. But you never had a problem playing anywhere, Yuni.'

Yuni smiled at Kazune's words. 'It only seemed like that. That's what you saw because that's what you wanted to see.'

Kazune looked surprised, so Yuni pressed on. 'You thought I was able to do things that didn't come so easily to you, right?'

Before Kazune could reply, Yuni sat down at the piano and opened the fallboard, straight away sounding some notes out on the keyboard.

I'll probably never forget that moment with the twins. Instinctively, it seemed, they looked each other in the eyes in perfect symmetry.

'It sounds great!' Yuni turned around, her eyes sparkling.

Thank God. I breathed a sigh of relief. I was nervous about Yuni, who could no longer play, sitting at the piano and striking the keys. My heart was in my mouth whenever I was in her company.

Kazune nodded. 'Yes, it does. It's perfect.' She too was smiling.

At this moment, I couldn't tell the difference between them.

'Kazune, the thing is' – Yuni's voice was cheerful – 'you can play fantastically well wherever you are.'

Yuni stood up and the two girls now exchanged places without fuss. Kazune spread out her sheet music on the stand and sat down. Just as Yuni had done, she struck a key with her finger. This must have been the standard A above middle C, but I could immediately picture scenery opening out before me, with a path extending through a crisp, silvery forest. A young deer seemed to frolic in a hidden glade.

Yuni gazed up at me, her face beaming. 'It sounds like the splashing of clear water.'

I was struck by how the same sound could conjure up entirely different images, depending on the person listening.

'I used this particular sound as the foundation for the entire tone and colour,' I explained, and Kazune nodded again.

She returned her hands to her lap for a moment, then slowly began to play her piece. It started so naturally I had no time to gather myself – as though she'd quietly latched on to music drifting about in the ether, and was channelling it for us through the piano. Her hands were sure and confident as they moved up and down the run of the keys, never faltering. When Kazune played, everything seemed heightened in its reality, as if the piano and the music had a life of their own.

Leisurely enough at the start, by halfway through the piece the sound was utterly sublime, with the notes lingering in the air like a cascade of sparkling gemstones, stretching as they emerged before fading away, as pure as can be, each tone in perfect harmony with the rest.

'It's completely different from when she practised at home,' Yuni said excitedly. 'So this is what you can do – to make it sound like this!' Face flushed, she turned to me. 'You are amazing, Mr Tomura. I can't wait to start learning how to tune. I want to be your apprentice.'

I fell silent. *Whaat?*

My voice was off-key. 'The amazing person here isn't me, it's Kazune.'

She had sounded out the possibilities at first, and now the instrument belonged to her. Just as Yuni had said, Kazune could adjust to playing any piano.

'Not at all – it's the tone of this piano pulling her along. Kazune's riding it, enjoying herself, drawing out sounds she's never dreamed of before.'

At that point a member of the restaurant staff appeared in the hall. 'Is it all right if we start getting things ready in here? We don't mind if you continue playing.'

'Yes, please go ahead,' I said.

I was glad we'd come early. Glad that she'd had time to try out the piano.

Several of the waiting staff appeared and began re-arranging the tables. Kazune, unperturbed by the commotion around her, played on.

'Mr Yanagi let her choose all the pieces, too,' Yuni whispered to me. 'The two of us talked it over a lot, wondering what sort of music would be appropriate for a wedding reception.'

'I'm sure it'll be perfect,' I said, and Yuni nodded. The second piece was baroque in style, an upbeat, fast-moving yet gentle piece. This wasn't a solo performance or competition entry, but music to add a touch of colour to Mr Yanagi's wedding reception. Gentle, pleasant pieces were just the thing, I reckoned. Just as I was thinking how great it all sounded, it happened.

What the—? I suddenly thought. I looked at the piano and at Kazune. She was still playing, a serene expression on her face. Beyond her, the staff were spreading pale pink cloths on the tables. Nothing about the piano or Kazune had changed over the last few minutes.

But something was bothering me. The sound was different – more muffled and less clear than before.

'Excuse me,' someone said from behind us. I turned to see another waiter passing by, arms full of tablecloths. I stood a little further away from the piano. Activity was picking up around the room. Kazune seemed to be playing just the same as before, but something had definitely shifted.

Was she holding back out of consideration for the restaurant which was now so busy? The sound was no longer reaching out. Before the fine vibrations had time to reach my ears, they were falling apart and scattering along the floor.

I approached the piano to check things out, but drew to a halt. There was no change to Kazune's playing. It was definitely the piano – the sound had no oomph to it and wasn't projecting. And what's more, the sound kept changing with each step as I drew closer to the piano. 'Excuse me. I need to check something.'

Kazune had finished, and turned to face me, hands in her lap.

'Did you change how you were playing, from the way you were in the beginning?' I asked, and she shook her head.

'Do you feel like the sound has changed?'

She gave a slight nod. 'All of a sudden it doesn't sing like it did before.'

She looked behind me and I followed her gaze. Yuni was at the back of the hall. She motioned her sister to play one more time.

Something wasn't right.

Eyes on Kazune, I moved away from the piano, slowly edging towards the first table. Making my way around the staff members, I moved to the next table, and then the next. The sound wandered, disordered and confused, bounced off the moving waiting staff and was absorbed by the spread-out tablecloths. I could feel this in my very skin. Suddenly I recalled how, in the twins' music room, it had seemed such a waste that the sound was deadened by the heavy cloth curtains.

I'd been careless and had barely considered the surroundings. I'd only worked with pianos in domestic homes and my inexperience showed. But this wasn't the time for regret and there was no time for introspection. I had to retune it. Oh, but how could I? There'd be more tablecloths, and the place would be full of guests, each of them reflecting or absorbing the sound. The ceaseless activity of staff bringing in and taking out food, the clatter of silverware against plates, people whispering to each other fond memories of the bride and groom . . . I needed to imagine all of this in order to adjust the sound. Would there be enough time? There had to be.

'Kazune, please let me adjust the piano a bit.'

She nodded, accommodating as ever.

'Kazune will be fine. She can play any piano anywhere,' Yuni said with a mischievous smile. I hated how tactless I was being.

'My apologies,' I said, bowing to the girls. I remembered how I'd bowed in apology to them before. How, while still a beginner, I'd thought I could tune their piano by myself but ended up unable to. Since then, nothing had changed. The only thing I had now was a little more technique, a little more experience and the determination to get things right at all costs.

'This might take a while, so why don't you find a corner to take a break and relax?' I bowed to them once more. I had no idea how long it would take, and more worryingly, there was no guarantee I'd even be able to do it.

'Mr Tomura,' Yuni said cheerfully, 'it'll be OK. I'll sit over there and you can transmit the sound in my direction.'

Transmit? Unable to fathom what she was saying, I must have looked perplexed. As Yuni walked to the back of the hall she said it in a different way.

'Umm, it'd be good to draw the sound out all the way over to here. That sound you're getting right now. *Draw out* – is that the right expression? Umm – *lift* the sound all the way over here!'

I couldn't help chuckling as she struggled to come up with the right word. 'Thank you.'

Transmit, draw out, lift. I knew what Yuni was trying to express. The question was how to produce it.

The vague words began to take shape. *Make it shine. Lift the sounds and make them shine* – that's what I had to do. The constellations. Tonight the ones you could see would be Ursa Minor, Ursa Major, Leo. No matter where you viewed them from, they shone high up in the sky, the outline of them eternal.

'Bright, quiet, crystal-clear writing.'

I murmured this to myself and stood ready in front of the piano.

∽

MY CONSTELLATION. ALWAYS THERE ABOVE the forest, and all I needed to do was head towards it.

As lovely as a dream, yet as exact as reality.

That was my constellation. I had to make it shine upon Kazune as she played, and Yuni, too, seated further off. I started by adjusting the depth of the pedals so that when Kazune depressed them the sound would resonate the way she wanted it to, and spread to each and every corner of this room. Next came the way the casters lay beneath the legs. Once, before a recital, Mr Itadori had changed the direction in which they faced in order to adjust the sound. Back then I'd merely watched, impressed. But now I understood: the centre of gravity was currently with the legs all facing inwards. Making them face outwards instead would bend the column plate to an infinitesimal degree, thereby changing how the sound radiated out. I had done all that I could.

∽

KAZUNE, RESPLENDENT IN A CHARTREUSE dress, began to play. This was less solemn, more rousing, and I barely recognized it – a wedding march. A celebratory piece to hail the happy couple. Kazune played the grace notes slowly, as if they were the melody. In a way this in itself was as lovely as a dream, as exact as reality. The bride and groom, joyful and beaming, made their entrance and everyone applauded. As they passed by the tables, they nodded shyly to those around them. Miss Hamano, the new bride, was radiant. She bowed to the surrounding guests as the couple made their way to the front of the room.

'Aren't weddings wonderful?' I couldn't help but whisper to Mr Akino beside me.

'You're gutsier than I imagined, Tomura.' He gave a forced smile. 'If it were me and the pianist was playing a piano I'd tuned, I'd be feeling pretty tense, not smiling and chatting like you're doing.'

Now that he mentioned it, I realized I wasn't tense at all. Kazune probably wasn't either. The light, cheerful sound continued. This was different from a concert. Neither the piano nor the pianist – let alone the tuner – were the lead players here, since this was Mr Yanagi and Miss Hamano's wedding reception. The salons of old might well have felt like this.

'I don't know, I just really like it.'

Mr Akino's mouth turned down at the corners for a moment.

'I suppose,' he admitted reluctantly, and then murmured, 'The piano sounds pretty good, doesn't it?'

I nodded, glancing across at Yuni. She was smiling, tears welling up in her eyes. What the tears meant, I had no idea. I couldn't fathom the emotions running through the twins as Yuni kept a close and loving eye on Kazune. All I could do was watch, bedazzled, as they smiled and cried, the piano always at the centre of their lives.

'You've never praised me before,' I said and glanced at Mr Akino beside me. He was back to looking blasé.

I wasn't sure if he was saying the tuning was good, or Kazune's playing, but it didn't matter. You couldn't say that one of these was good without the other.

'Kazune's playing so beautifully,' Yuni said in a tearful voice. 'She's celebrating Mr Yanagi's marriage, saying congratulations to them. It sounds that way, don't you think?'

Congratulations? Maybe. But it seemed a little softer than that to me. It was so gentle, so exquisite, going straight to the heart in a way that nearly made me cry.

I nodded emphatically. 'Kazune is absolutely going to be a great pianist.'

Even if you didn't know anything about music you were helplessly drawn in as she played. Even if you decided not to listen, not to notice it, you couldn't help but look up. That was the power of Kazune's playing. In her hands, she could express joy or sadness with a single note, all seemingly without effort. Never showy, always gentle – the particles of sound were so fine they sank directly into the heart, and stayed there.

When you heard Kazune play, it summoned up visible, tangible scenery. Light shining down among the trees, wet with morning dew. Drops of water sparkling on the tips of leaves, then dripping down. One morning, repeated over and over again. A vibrancy and solemnity born fresh and new.

It was true, I decided. She really was sending out her congratulations.

Kazune's playing was a celebration of life.

'You said *absolutely*,' Mr Akino whispered.

'Yes.'

'You maintain there's no such thing as an absolute sound, yet you just said Kazune will *absolutely* become a great pianist. Well,' he went on, 'I would have to agree with you.'

∽

WE GATHERED TO EAT, AND all my colleagues from the company were seated together.

I was thrilled that a piano I had tuned could sound so good. I'd previously thought that if another tuner could coax an even better sound from a piano, I'd have no problem in handing over the reins. For the sake of the instrument, for the person playing, for all those enjoying the music.

But now I felt differently. I wanted to tune Kazune's piano. I wanted to make it better. I wanted it to be me at the reins.

Tuning accomplished on whose behalf? Who was it I wanted to make happy?

Kazune, of course.

I loved her playing, and I'd tried to ensure this piano gave full voice to the beauty of her performance. In that moment, I had had neither Mr Yanagi nor the wedding guests in mind. All I had thought of was Kazune's playing.

Which I now realized was a mistake – I should have thought of the guests as well, considered the size of the room and the height of the ceiling. The front seats, the seats at the back, the middle seats, near the door – how many people would be there, and where. I should have imagined in advance how the sound would project, so that it would reach each and every one of them in equal measure.

Up until now I'd only tuned pianos in people's homes. And that wouldn't do if I wanted to tune Kazune's piano. I finally understood that. I'd been so sure I wasn't going to aim at being a concert piano tuner, and it had been a mistake to think in that way.

'It'd be good to check that the dampers are all coming down as one.' Mr Itadori's voice was cool, yet his words were firm. I'd adjusted the pedals so the dampers would all lift together, but hadn't thought about the way they'd come down.

'You need to assist Kazune in bringing out the very best qualities in her performance,' he added.

'You're absolutely right.'

When she had played the piano in our little auditorium at the showroom, the chords she had produced were exquisite. My conjecture had been that she had enhanced the sound through her pedal technique. And I was right.

I trembled at the thought that I had learned something new. (One truly can tremble with excitement, it turns out.) I'd adjusted the pedals so they would be a touch more sensitive. Any more and they'd be too responsive. Yet Mr Itadori was telling me to make them even more precise.

'I think you should trust Kazune more.'

'I know.'

He trusted Kazune, and at this moment I felt as though he trusted me, too.

'That's part of our job as tuners, too, to nurture pianists.'

Later, when she took a break from playing, I'd adjust the pedals for maximum sensitivity. I'd been told how humiliating it was to retune a piano in the middle of a performance, but I didn't care. All I cared about was helping Kazune produce the most beautiful, memorable sound she could.

'I wonder if maybe . . .' Mr Akino began. 'If maybe someone like Tomura might actually get there.'

Someone like Tomura? What kind of person did he mean? And get *where*?

'I think you're right.' The MD was leaning over to eavesdrop on our conversation. 'I always thought it odd that someone like you would become a tuner. I wondered why Mr Itadori had recommended you so highly.'

So Mr Itadori *had* recommended me? I thought they hired on a first-come, first-served basis.

'What do you mean – someone like me?' I asked.

'How should I put it? A person who was raised, well . . . someone with an upbringing like yours.'

Miss Kitagawa had said the same thing to me before. And I don't think she had meant it as a compliment. It felt as if she meant someone bland and boring.

'But now I think someone like Tomura is the type who can make his way, very patiently, persistently, step by step, through the forest of wool and steel.'

'I think you're right,' Mr Itadori agreed generously. 'Because Tomura lived in the mountains, and the forest raised him.'

'This is delicious!' Miss Kitagawa suddenly said loudly, interrupting everyone. '*Oh – sorry!*' she said and looked down.

'The soup? It really is scrumptious.' This came from Yuni, chiming in.

Thanks to which, the echoes of Mr Itadori's comment faded away before I could really ruminate on it. Lived in the mountains, raised by the forest. Was that the case?

The idea made me deeply happy. Clearly a forest had been growing within me as well.

Perhaps I hadn't taken the wrong path after all. Even if it took time, even if there were detours, this was exactly the right path for me. I had thought there was nothing in the forest, nothing in the scenery around me, but now I knew: everything was there. It wasn't that it was hidden, but that I simply hadn't seen it.

Relief washed over me.

'Do you know something?' Miss Kitagawa wiped her mouth with a white napkin. 'There's lots of sheep farming where you grew up, isn't there? I was thinking how the Chinese character for *good* or *excellent*, 善, contains the character for *sheep*, 羊.'

'Really?'

'And I read recently how the character for *beauty*, too, 美, is derived from the character for sheep.'

She contemplated this for a while, and then added, as though further details had come back to her, 'In ancient China, sheep were like the gold standard for everything. They were sacrificed to the gods, too. Isn't that what you are always doing? Doing your utmost to find the good? The beautiful? When I realized that all of these words are derived from sheep, I thought — you know what? They're already there, *inside* the piano, from the very start.'

She was right. From the very beginning, the good and the beautiful are already there — inside that mighty, gleaming instrument.

I looked over and saw that Kazune was just beginning another piece. And it was indeed beautiful and right.

NATSU MIYASHITA was born in Fukui Prefecture on Honshu island, Japan, in 1967. She has had a lifelong passion for reading and writing and has played the piano since she was very young. *The Forest of Wool and Steel* has won several prizes in Japan – including the prestigious Japan Booksellers' Award, in which booksellers vote for the title they most enjoy selling in store – and became a bestseller. It has also been turned into a popular Japanese film directed by Kojiro Hashimoto and starring Kento Yamazaki.

PHILIP GABRIEL is an experienced translator from Japanese, and best known for his translation work with Haruki Murakami.

NATSU MIYASHITA was born in Fukui Prefecture on Honshu island, Japan, in 1967. She has had a lifelong passion for reading and writing and has played the piano since she was very young. *The Forest of Wool and Steel* has won several prizes in Japan – including the prestigious Japan Booksellers' Award, in which booksellers vote for the title they most enjoy selling in store – and became a bestseller. It has also been turned into a popular Japanese film directed by Kojiro Hashimoto and starring Kento Yamazaki.

PHILIP GABRIEL is an experienced translator from Japanese, and best known for his translation work with Haruki Murakami.